## UNDER ATTACK . . .
## NO BACK-UP, NO MERCY

Thornton kept the Browning's trigger depressed. The vintage weapon was singing now, Raven pouring more oil across the barrel as Bo fed the tray with one hand, traversing the gun with the other as he fed a steady stream of man-killers into the killing ground to his front. A dull *thud!* announced a grenade of some sort going off at the base of the protective wall below them, smoke and splinters of plaster shooting straight upward and showering the defenders with debris. Bo had no idea how the fight was going elsewhere, the team essentially cut off from the rest of the compound as the battle's ferocity grew.

"I got through to the embassy!" yelled Captain Travers as he flopped down beside Thornton, M-16 in hand. "Advised them we were under heavy attack and requested support. Ain't nothing available."

"Can't they divert a jet or two our way?" barked Thornton.

"Don't count on it."

# STORMING IRAQ
## GREG WALKER

JOVE BOOKS, NEW YORK

STORMING IRAQ

A Jove Book / published by arrangement with
the author

PRINTING HISTORY
Jove edition / March 1992

ISBN: 0-515-10762-X

Jove Books are published by The Berkley Publishing Group,
200 Madison Avenue, New York, New York 10016.
The name "JOVE" and the "J" logo
are trademarks belonging to Jove Publications, Inc.

PRINTED IN THE UNITED STATES OF AMERICA

10  9  8  7  6  5  4  3  2  1

## DEDICATION

For my editor, Jeff Hardwick, who cut me slack when I fell behind the power curve.

For the guys of ODA 152.

For the Kurdish people, who died for our sins.

For those operators who paid the ultimate price.

This last one's for you.

—Greg Walker
Bend, Oregon
22 April 91

# CHAPTER

## 1

Iraq's dark coastline off her port side, the USS *Curtis* slipped quietly through the softly rolling waters of the Persian Gulf. An antisubmarine warfare escort, the *Curtis* was from the *Oliver Hazard Perry* class, a distinction which allowed her an antiair capability as well. But tonight she was engaged in a completely different kind of operation. Below decks a flurry of last-minute activity was taking place as a platoon of SEALs prepared to go ashore once again. With the ground war in Kuwait less than twenty-four hours old, coalition forces had successfully breached the defensive lines built by Iraqi forces over a six-month period of time. The frigate *Curtis* was assigned the designator "ST-38," meaning she was involved with the transport, delivery, support, and recovery of Special Operations forces with targets in Iraq. A combined UDT/SEAL unit had been working the beaches and inner waterways since the early days of the war. Also on board was another team, a team which officially did not, could not, exist. Its commander was a man named Thornton. Its mission was to kick ass and take names.

"Here's your AK, twelve magazines with full loads just like you ordered." Sergeant-Major Frank Hartung (ret.) adjusted his feet as the ship's bow burst through a wall of water. The impact of steel meeting wave sent a gentle shudder through the frigate's guts. Dressed in well-worn camouflage pants and a black T-shirt, Hartung was busy finalizing the team's equipment issue before launch time. A combat veteran of more than one war, Frank Hartung had served alongside Thornton when the two were assigned to Combat Control North (CCN) in Vietnam.

Finished with lacing up his soft-soled jungle boots, Beaumont "Bo" Thornton gratefully accepted the Russian assault rifle and its magazine-laden chest harness. "Thanks, Frank. How's the team looking?"

"Good, real good. Jason did a commo check with the C&C center; no problem there. Mike, Lee, and Alan spent time with the SEALs going in before us, just to ensure everyone was working off the same sheet of music. Cal's topside; seems Conrad blasted us a message they're busy decoding right now. We launch in an hour, providing Murphy doesn't poke his nose into things."

Nodding, Bo quickly ran the AK through a function check. Satisfied with the weapon's performance, he set it aside, drawing his Browning Hi-Power from a soft leather shoulder holster strapped under his left armpit. The Browning had been with the former Green Beret since his first tour of Vietnam with Project B-52. It was an old and trusted friend. "Heard the SEALs lasered a few more of old Saddam's high-rises last night. Can't be much of Baghdad standing, given the pounding they've been taking lately."

Taking a spot across from Thornton, Hartung sat down. They were in a portion of the ship which was off-limits to all but a handful of officers and SEAL commandos. Officially Springblade was no more. The President had issued orders to disband the project after being tipped off that certain members of the government were plotting to kill Thornton and Company for a number of ill-advised reasons. But the fast-paced events which led to a declaration of war in the Gulf had pushed the team's evolution ahead of its schedule. The code name "Camelot" was assigned, and King George's men were buried deep now within the guts of Special Operations. Now on salary, Bo Thornton and his covey of hand-picked specialists found themselves shipping out for the Middle East. Their first mission had been to rescue hostages taken by Hussein's forces in Kuwait City. Successful, they'd been at sea ever since, supporting the Navy's over-the-beach efforts as requested.

"Yeah, the crazy bastards dressed up in some Iraqi uniforms they 'liberated,' dyed their skin and hair, then marched right down the main street of Baghdad like they owned the place. From there they broke up into squads, located their targets, then just sat back and painted those bad boys for the Air Force. Damned hand-held lasers sure work good; wish we'd had 'em in Nam."

Thornton grunted his agreement. They'd had beacons at CCN, but nothing like today's directional gear. Then again, the SMART bombs being dropped by the Air Force were supposed to be 900 percent more accurate than what was available in Vietnam, allowing for precision bombing with a minimum of noncombatant casualties. "Damned SEALs are as crazy today as they were in the Delta. Takes guts, balls, and some serious self-confidence to pull an op like that. Calvin's wishing he was still running with the pack, you can see it in his eyes every time they suit up."

Pulling a thick cigar from his cargo pocket, Hartung lit up. "Yeah, it's hard to get away from it once you've been there. Civilian life is flat-assed boring after the pump you get from doing what we've done for a living. We're a breed apart, Thornton, and I for one don't give a rat's big black ass what the nine-to-fivers think of us." Smiling, Frank blew a perfectly round smoke ring into the air between the two men.

"Who's flying tonight's sortie?" asked Bo.

"SEALs get a pair of F-15 Eagles off the *Midway*. They're going back up the Euphrates to paint some pontoon bridges the Iraqis threw up after the permanent structures came down last week."

"Should be fun," commented Thornton as he checked the Browning's magazine one last time. Satisfied, the big commando slammed the full box back up the automatic's

well, and the solid *click!* of the magazine catch spring-
ing into place told him the weapon was securely loaded.
"Who's playing with us?"

"Got a Wobbly Goblin with SMART bombs out of
'Somewhere In Saudi Arabia,' " replied Hartung. "Wobbly Goblin" was a nickname for the Lockheed F-117A
Stealth Fighter, whose birthplace was the "Skunk Works"
in Burbank, California. Begun in 1978, the F-117A was
designed to fly unseen by enemy radar as well as by
the human eye. Configured like a huge arrowhead, the
aircraft was operated by a single pilot using fly-by-wire
controls. This system, along with the odd shape necessary
for the plane's near-invisibility, demanded a sophisticated
on-board computer which aided the pilot in flying the
aircraft.

"Heard that hummer was kicking Saddam's ass all over
Iraq," said Bo. "Fifty-two-thousand-foot ceiling, top speed
of Mach 0.9, twelve-hundred-fifty-mile range, we're talking about a serious aircraft here."

Frank agreed. "You boys just need to get your lasers on
target and grab a hole. 'The Bear' got hard intel about
some Zodiacs with Exocet missiles mounted on them and
he wants them taken out. The freaking Iraqi Navy may
try and use them pups against one of the battle groups
in the AO and the last thing we need is a repeat of the
*Stark*."

"Roger that," growled Thornton, remembering the inci-
dent when an Iraqi jet blasted a hole large enough to drive
a compact car through in the USS *Stark*, killing more than
thirty sailors. Hussein claimed it was an accident; the
Iran-Iraq war was in full swing at the time. "We'll take
our 'rubber duck' into the mouth of the Euphrates, and
beach 'em just south of Al Faw where the Zodiacs are
supposed to be tied up. It's not much of a hump, according
to the strip map the UDT guys came up with, plenty of
cover to lay up sorry in until zero hour."

"Who's with the raft for security?" asked Frank.

"Be Mike and Jason. Alan's with me, he'll do the actual
targeting while I pull watch for any bad guys who get too

close. Easy in, easy out. Piece of cake op any way you cut it."

"My ass," warned Hartung. "We've been lucky so far and you damn well know it. Official policy is to deny S.O. casualties, but Sergeant Major Kelly with the Fifth told me they'd lost four chasing SCUD launchers two weeks ago. There's a DELTA team missing as well, some go-to-hell mission up in northern Iraq. They ain't carrying them boys MIA either, Bo. Guess that says it all, eh?"

Thornton's dark brown eyes were hard as he spoke. "I hear what you're saying, Frank. We'll be careful out there, count on it." Tugging his fully loaded combat harness, Bo slipped the safety strap from his combat knife's sheath, pulled the long tapered blade free and slid it lightly down the outside of his hairy forearm. Long, thick strands of hair literally popped into the air as the razor-sharp edge cut through their bases just above the roots.

"Now that's a new one," exclaimed Frank in admiration.

"Bob Rippy out of Texas made it for me. Natural linen Micarta handle shaped kinda like a coke bottle for a really secure grip, even if your hands and the knife are wet. Blade's ground outta ATS-34 steel, triple-quenched in liquid nitrogen and hand-sharpened. Gotta slight reverse curve to the primary edge for constant blade contact with whatever I'm cutting into, and the false edge is sharpened as well for delivering a backstroke. Single edge, single guard, all the fixtures made outta 303 stainless steel. Bob made me two, this one from three-sixteenth-inch stock as a fighter, the other from quarter-inch steel."

"Thicker stock for a camp knife, eh?" offered Frank.

"Roger that," confirmed Bo. "I told Rippy I wanted something that balanced on the pommel, which this thing does if you sit it up on a flat surface. The blade shape is almost like one of them Stealth Fighters you were taking about. Real lean and mean, meant for getting into the throat fast. With all the protective vests we're seeing these days it's pretty hard to attack the kidneys, so going back up top seems advisable."

Hartung accepted the offered blade from Thornton's hand. It was light for its size, and nicely balanced. "That's a killing knife if I've ever held one," complimented the sergeant-major. "You make sure you don't lose it like that Randall of yours!"

"Don't remind me." Thornton coughed. In a flash of recollection Bo relived the nightmare of Angel Barahone. His failure to replace the Randall's faulty sheath had resulted in the knife's loss at the worse time possible. Only fate had decreed Barahone hadn't seen the knife. A Sandinista chopper crew had recovered it after nearly spotting the two-man American team.

Glancing at his watch, Frank slapped both knees and stood. "Enough jaw-jacking, we gotta get the team together. You got forty minutes before this old tub's in position; the SEALs shove off in twenty. Anything I ought to know before you insert?"

Bo studied his friend, noting the deepening wrinkles around the eyes and nose, the square cut of Hartung's jaw as it chomped down on the still-burning cigar, the cast of his intense eyes under their bushy brows. Frank Hartung was his closest friend as well as one of the best operators he'd known since donning the beret. "You remember where the letter to Linda is, right?"

"Sure, in your footlocker like always."

"I get tagged and bagged . . ."

"You get zapped and I'll make sure the girl's taken care of," responded Frank. "Lin's become like a daughter to me, you know that. Just worry about the assholes in the boat with you. I'll make sure the wife makes out okay if the man upstairs yanks your chain."

"Tell her I love her, she needs to know that, to believe it."

"You'll tell her yourself, partner. Now quit this John Wayne shit and let's get loaded up. The boys are waitin' on us on deck!"


When Saddam Hussein invaded Kuwait he threw not only the United States but the whole world off-center. A respectable tyrant in the Middle East, Hussein had seized the reins of power in Iraq the old-fashioned way—by killing for them. His own country was a mixture of Islamic rivalries and tribal disputes, and Hussein had enforced his rule through mass murder and intricate political maneuverings. With the war with Iran he set forth to conquer his most deadly and powerful enemy (besides the Jews of Israel). It would take eight years of wholesale slaughter before Saddam's legions were battled to a standstill. In the meantime he'd used chemical weapons against both the Iranians and his own subjects, thumbing his nose at the world when it sought to condemn his violations of the Geneva Conventions, to which Iraq was a signatory.

Its economy shaken to the core by war and despoiled by Hussein's own robbing of the country's coffers, Iraq had faced a growing number of internal problems that Saddam was incapable of solving through peaceful means. The diversion of millions of dollars into the hands of the military was crippling the internal development of the country, especially after Iraq's war with Iran—huge amounts of Hussein's arsenal had been gobbled up in the maelstrom of that pointless confrontation. In a frenzy to rebuild his protective ring of armor and air forces, Saddam gambled on the international oil market and ranted against his neighbor Kuwait, which insisted on producing more oil than OPEC's agreed-upon limits. Oil was money to Hussein, and money was needed to prop up Iraq's increasing instability.

Finally Hussein fell back on historical grounds to justify an armed assault against Kuwait. Claiming the country was actually Iraq's nineteenth province until it was sliced away by Britain, Saddam further charged Kuwait with stealing oil from Iraq via the shared field which straddled both countries. In addition, Hussein demanded to lease two barren islands belonging to Kuwait, islands that essentially blocked Iraq's unlimited (and unobserved) use of the Persian Gulf through the Shatt al Arab. Kuwait rejected all of the claims, charges, and demands levied by Hussein, never believing he would resort to military force.

But the "Butcher of Baghdad" did. In a combined armor and air campaign, Iraq poured over 100,000 troops into Kuwait, driving its army out and forcing the government into a hasty exile in Saudi Arabia. Hussein ignored warnings from the United States. Why should he listen to a country which had compromised with the North Koreans, negotiated with the Cubans, been forced to withdraw by the Vietnamese, cowered before the Iranians, and had been unable to pull off the invasion of two small Central American countries? Saddam was also relying on the Arab countries to resist allowing such a great infidel as the United States to place troops on their sacred soil. He would call for a holy war, bringing the "Mother of All Battles" home to the hearts and minds of the American people.

But the plan backfired.

Not only did America step forward, so did thirty-eight other countries. Saudi Arabia hosted the coalition's forces, and Egypt and Syria backed the allies. The United Arab Emirates, Oman, and Qatar joined forces with the United States, perhaps foreseeing that Kuwait's fate would be their own if Hussein went unchallenged. Turkey sealed her northern border with Iraq, giving coalition forces secure air bases from which to mount devastating attacks against Baghdad and other strategic targets. Kuwait herself was resisting. Tiny bands of armed men and women were killing the invader wherever he was found, providing intelligence on his positions and movements, and vowing to take their country back regardless of the costs involved.

When the ground war began, the unsuspected and underrated force of the United States was the sharpened tip of the coalition sword. Iraq, already reeling from unprecedented bombing attacks, was herself under siege, as hundreds of Special Forces operators happily romped through her backyard. It was for freedom they fought, it was for freedom they were dying.

Saddam Hussein had fucked up once too many times, according to Bo Thornton. Payback, like the man said, was a motherfucker.

• • •

The black rubber raft's engine expertly muffled, they motored most of the way in. Dark waves smacked against the sides of the tiny craft, and its bow blasted through them, showering the men huddled inside with wet sea-spray.

Their departure from the *Curtis* had been uneventful. The SEALs had launched earlier, because their target was farther upriver. It was a quiet night. For the most part, the war was raging farther south, although Baghdad would once again be taking a beating from the Air Force. Thornton, hunkered down in the bow, was reminded of his many practice missions as a young ranger, in boats much like the one taking them ashore this night. But the coast of Iraq was a far more hostile shore than that of Santa Rosa Island, where blanks and "arty" simulators were the order of the day.

Their mission was to seek out the Iraqi Zodiacs, which were reported to be outfitted with Exocet missiles, rockets capable of sinking any of the fleet's ships steaming the Gulf just off Saddam's shores. Knowing the dictator wouldn't hesitate to order his sailors to attack, General Norman Schwarzkopf had directed the Special Ops Command to find the seaborne launch platforms first, then to destroy them. It was bad enough that the ocean was littered with hastily dropped mines; the thought of suicidal navy commandos ripping across the open waters with an armed and ready Exocet was simply too much to bear. Bo tucked his wet AK in closer to his side, pleased that the "wet suit" he'd rigged from a condom seemed to be keeping the ocean's spray off the laser he'd mounted before departing the ship.

"Mouth of the river coming up!" hissed Mike Bannion. Thornton nodded, gripping the assault rifle tighter, as they neared the dark maw of the Euphrates. From what the intel people reported, the "Zods," as the SEALs called them, weren't too far up the river. If there were sentries posted anywhere nearby, the frogmen would have run into them first, which obviously hadn't happened, given the gloomy shroud of silence surrounding the invaders.

"Tell Silver to cut the engine," whispered Thornton. "We'll use the paddles from here on out."

In a moment the powerful motor ceased to operate, and the raft turned slightly sideways as the river's outgoing current began to turn the blunt rubber nose away from its goal. "Stroke, you assholes!" grunted Bannion. "Let's get in closer to the shore where there's at least some cover." As one the men leaned into their task, the raft began to make headway as their powerful strokes pushed it deeper into the guts of Iraq.

Thirty minutes later Alan Rowe tapped a sweating Bo Thornton on the shoulder. "Grab us some sand, boss. Coordinates put the bad guys about a hundred meters upriver. We'll be walking from here on in." Refolding the waterproofed map, Rowe slipped it inside his fatigue shirt and began paddling as Jason turned them toward the shoreline from his position at the tiller. With a soft *crunnnch* they went aground. Mike Bannion slipped over the slick side of the raft, grasping the bowline and pulling the craft further up the beach. The barrel of Thornton's AK swung lazily to and fro; Bo's job was to provide suppressive fire should they have landed in the wrong place at the right time.

The beach was abandoned.

"Ought to be someone here," offered Rowe.

"They're supposed to be tucked up in a tributary, laying low and waiting for old Saddam to order their asses to sea. Probably fast asleep, considering there's been no activity around here for several weeks," answered Mike.

"Let's get moving," ordered Bo. "The SEALs got past them or we'd have heard about it by now. If they're slackin' off it's a lick on 'em. Hand me my ruck, will ya, Al?"

Minutes later the raft was firmly ashore, and a dark camouflage net had been thrown over it to break up its distinctive outline. Silver, his face darkened and his hands full of 5.56 firepower, sent a burst to the *Curtis* via SatCom radio. "They know we're in position," he told the others. "The flyboy is upstairs just waiting for us to paint pretty pictures, and everything's still a 'go' according to Cal."

Thornton nodded. He had to admit he was impressed by the hardware and thought which were guiding their missions. Hussein's boys were getting creamed behind the lines; tiny teams of night fighters were blasting them out of their positions at every turn. For a country with the fourth largest army in the world, Iraq was proving to be remarkably inept at taking on anything but token Resistance forces. *Love to have a military surplus store here after the war*, Bo thought to himself. "Jay, you stay by the radio like we planned. Mike's got the beach; anything that ain't us goes down hard. Al and me gonna take a little walk and see if we can locate these jerks. I'll call ya when we're ready, okay?"

Silver gave a curt thumbs-up. A lightweight set of earphones in his ears, he hunkered down by the raft and adjusted the radio's volume.

"I'll be up on that dune over there," said Bannion, pointing to a nearby hill of sand. "Should be able to cover you for a fair distance should the shit hit the fan." Smiling, the DEA SLAM agent hefted a scoped M-14A1 rifle to his shoulder. The SEALs had opted to return to the heavier but more powerful rifle, forsaking the M-16 as too fragile for their uses. Beach security demanded fast, accurate, powerful firepower. The M-14 could deliver, and Bannion could shoot.

"Let's do it," ordered Bo. "I'll provide security for Al once we're on-site. He's gonna survey the base, locate the targets, then lay out his gear. Tell that pilot to lay his ordnance in carefully; we're not gonna be that far away. Last thing I want to do is go home a KIA due to 'friendly fire.'"

"Roger that," agreed Silver. "I'll keep him honest, Bo. You dudes be careful, the Iraqis might actually have someone on guard tonight."

" . . . or up beatin' his meat," quipped Mike.

"I'm ready," said Rowe.

High overhead a spy satellite began snapping pictures of the team's target area, its heat-sensitive film ready to receive whatever damage Thornton & Company might be able to inflict on the sleeping Iraqi sailors and their deadly missiles.

"Use the 9-mm," ordered Bo. Adjusting the focus on his NVG goggles, the powerful commando leader rechecked the single Iraqi soldier sitting silently on the sand not more than twenty feet from where he and Alan Rowe were hiding. The two men had experienced no trouble locating the Zodiacs; the smell of freshly brewed coffee had drawn the night stalkers in like fish on a line. *The enemy's security sucks*, thought Bo. *You can dress 'em up like soldiers but . . .*

His thoughts were interrupted by Rowe. "Ready."

"Do him!"

The *pppffft* of a subsonic round leaving its rifled hideaway caused but a ripple in the night's calm. The dozing guard's head jerked hard under the impact of the bullet. Brain matter sprayed the light brown sand around him as bits of bone whistled through the air. The body slowly keeled over to its right, settling onto the cool earth as life ebbed away with only the man's killers as an audience.

"Nice shot," congratulated Bo under his breath.

"Easy target," replied Alan as he tucked the black automatic into its holster. "These guys must think they're leading charmed lives, not to be taking better precautions than this."

"Underpaid and overrated. Everyone forgets Israel has kicked ass on her neighbors since the Jewish State was announced. Hussein's thugs have all the toys, but they ain't first-rate soldiers. Let's get into position and finish the job."

Minutes later the two men found their targets. The all-black Zodiacs lay bobbing like plump corks in the slow-running water of the tributary, their snouts tethered to the shore by thick lengths of nylon rope. From where he lay Thornton could see the missile launchers, each destructive probe covered by thick canvas. The Iraqis had mounted the missiles so that each Zodiac was capable of firing a rocket in a 360-degree arc. The coalition's fear was that these low-profile raiders of the sea would be ordered into the Gulf to attack U.S. ships, including the aircraft carriers supporting the air-ground war. The Exocet was a weapon to be feared, and one which might not be avoided if a volley of the French rockets were unleashed during one massed assault.

"I'm ready to paint," whispered Rowe.

"Go ahead," replied Bo. "Nothing seems to be moving. Let's get the lasers in place and call in the Goblin."

Nodding, Alan pulled three small plastic boxes from his claymore bag. Each instrument was capable of emitting a pencil-thin laser beam, a beam which the F-117A's pilot could "read" using the sophisticated equipment built into the plane's cramped cockpit. Each SMART bomb on board was set to ride an invisible signal down onto the designated target, with accuracy guaranteed up to one meter of ground zero. Rowe's job was to set up a triangle of lasers so that each beam would meet at the target's center point. Once activated, the beacon would serve as a bull's-eye for the Goblin's arsenal.

"We're still lookin' good, Al. Get them pups in place and let's move out. I'm getting a spooky feeling about this dump!"

Rowe smiled, his white teeth sparkling in the desert's dim moonlight. "Roger that. But if you think it's weird now, just wait 'til the Goblin gets on-station. He'll drop from about twelve thousand AGL and these poor bastards won't even know what hit them."

Bo chuckled under his breath. Rowe was right. The Stealth program had been ridiculed as too much money for an unproven technology by its critics, critics who were now probably wishing they'd not gone on record. Thornton knew the Wobbly Goblins ruled the air over Kuwait and Iraq, dropping their ordnance when and wherever they pleased, with no casualties. "Get moving," he ordered Rowe, "and don't bring anyone back to meet Mom, okay?"

Like a ghost, the newest member of the Springblade team vanished into the night. Only the slightest whisper of his uniform brushing against the earth betrayed any hint of movement, even to Thornton's keen ear.

Bo settled in, adjusting his body to the lay of the ground. Somewhat comfortable he brought a handheld NVG to his eye, sweeping the surrounding area for intruders. The device illuminated the target site clearly, revealing only the lumps of equipment stored nearby and Alan's crawling form. It was odd watching his comrade moving about so carefully when Bo could easily see him; the science of modern-day warfare took all the mystery out of the craft. Thornton was pleased to know the Iraqis didn't possess the same capability. If they did, the game would have different rules.

A shimmer of movement caught his eye. Off to the left flank someone was walking toward the Zodiacs, a rifle slung casually across his shoulder. Without hesitation Bo slipped his Browning free and rapidly screwed a short suppressor onto the threaded ends of its specially milled barrel. Lowering his head-mounted NVG into position, the big commando activated the device and took aim on the meddler. The Browning was equipped with a set of night sights that glowed nicely in the green-and-black environment of the NVG's scope. The man's path was on a collision course with Rowe, who was planting one of the lasers near a jumble of fifty-five-gallon fuel drums. If Alan was aware of the soldier's presence he must have been expecting Thornton to take care of the problem.

Slipping the hammer back, Bo braced himself for the shot. He now had a clear view of the man's chest. The front sight was riding just below the base of the target's throat. A few more steps and he'd be on top of Rowe, who had just rolled silently next to one of the drums. Thornton allowed himself a moment to inwardly relax, then squeezed the trigger.

As if hit with a baseball bat, the soldier staggered, then fell. Rowe was up and moving. Thornton caught a glint of silver in Rowe's hand as the commando's combat knife ripped through the air and into the dying man's body. Better safe than sorry, mused Bo as the ghastly scene was played out before his goggled eyes. Finished with his kill, Rowe dragged the body off the narrow path, stuffing it next to a pile of empty wooden crates. Then he was up and moving again, headed toward the final point of the triangle where the last laser was to be emplaced. Thornton was again scanning the AO, hoping no other Iraqis would come looking for their deceased Islamic brother.

The area was clear. Only the normal sounds of a base camp at rest disturbed the quiet of the desert.

Ten minutes later Rowe was back. "They're armed and sending. Let's get a move on in case our flyboy wants to get home early!"

"Nice job on the trooper," commented Bo drily. "How was my aim?"

"Good enough for government work. He was still breathing coming down, but I took care of that, as you probably saw."

"That blade is a damned sharp piece. Where'd you pick it up?"

"One of the boys from DELTA traded it to me before we flew out to the *Curtis*. They got forty of them to try out. He wanted to keep his but I had a goodie from the old days he couldn't pass up. The knife went through our dead guy like a fist through fog; my compliments to its maker."

Thornton slapped the former beret lightly on the shoulder. "Better go now. Mike and Jason are most likely getting edgy as hell waiting for us to return. When's the Stealth supposed to drop?"

Checking his watch, Rowe held up ten fingers twice. Both men grunted and began scrambling back toward the river. Thornton took point. His Browning out and held low, Bo wasted no time getting back to safety. If anyone had been between him and Rowe, the man would have died quickly and without question.

"Let's go!" hissed Thornton as Mike Bannion returned the One-Zero's single burst of pen-gun light with two of his own. "Get the raft out in the water and let's use the engine. The Goblin should be lining up on our beacon right about now." All four men hurriedly threw their equipment into the boat, grasping its hard rubber handles and lifting it free of the hard-packed sand. Running, they splashed into the shallow water of the river's edge, not letting the raft float free until they were waist-deep. As Bo covered the team with his 9-mm, each man pulled himself aboard to take up a security position. With a soft grunt, Silver manhandled Thornton over the slippery bow, then fired the engine with a mighty tug of the starter rope.

Grasping the tiller, the former ranger turned the boat on its heel, goosing the throttle so the bow lifted clean out of the water. Getting clear was the only thing that mattered now, because a duo of 2000-pound SMART bombs were headed downrange within minutes. The others were packed tightly into the guts of the raft, their weapons pointed over the sides and into the darkness. The *Curtis* had been informed by Silver that they were en route back, and Cal was standing by to take them aboard once they were safely back in the Gulf.

Without warning a massive eruption of flame exploded up from the place where the Iraqi camp was hidden, followed immediately by secondary explosions, as gasoline and ammunition detonated. A series of heavy blasts told the commandos that the Exocets were adding to the damage. A hot orange glow confirmed that the mission had been accomplished.

"Not bad for a bunch of old guys," quipped Jason.

"Airborne and amen," added Bo.

On shore an Iraqi patrol returning to their encampment stared silently at the fiercely burning maelstrom just over a klick away from their position. With a grunt the patrol leader signaled a halt. He would wait until daylight to return, knowing there was nothing to be done until then. Besides, where there was one American patrol there might be others, and he was in no mood to run into who was lurking around in Saddam's backyard.

Allah be praised.

# CHAPTER
## 2

Colonel Ali ibn el Hussein grimaced as yet another volley of enemy shells exploded on the outskirts of the city. Glancing out the huge window of his upstairs head-quarters, he watched the lazy black plumes of smoke billow upward into the sky, tiny fingers of orange fire barely visible at their bases. The coalition's accuracy was improving with every hour, he thought. Forward observers were clearly in the area, which meant either the Resist-ance or Army Special Forces teams. Hussein snapped his fingers at a nearby orderly, and the man quickly crossed the carpeted floor to where the powerfully built colonel stood.

"Tell my staff it is time to depart by whatever means are available," he told the soldier. "I want Sergeant Mirza's men downstairs in ten minutes with the cars. Also, send Captain Ibrahim to me. Now go!"

The man stiffened, saluted, then turned and jogged to the open door leading out of the littered office. He would find Ibrahim first, knowing he was the officer in charge of executions. The colonel obviously wanted the prison-ers locked downstairs to be done away with before the Americans arrived in force. Mirza, the sergeant in charge of Hussein's handpicked and Russian-trained personal bodyguard, would be next. As he began loping toward the captain's cramped office the soldier prayed he wouldn't be left behind to fend for himself. The Kuwaitis would be hunting Iraqi soldiers in earnest, now that the "Mother of All Battles" was turning into the Mother of All Defeats.

Alone again Hussein forced himself to consider the situation calmly. Seven months ago he'd accepted his cousin's challenge to obliterate the Kuwaiti state and absorb its wealth and culture into the glory of a new and more powerful Iraq. His success had been impressive: the entire city was stripped of anything valuable, all of it forwarded to Baghdad in convoy after convoy of heavily laden trucks. Of course the infidels had raged against the so-called "looting" of the nineteenth province, not realizing that, as part of Iraq, the former country of Kuwait possessed nothing which did not belong to President Hussein's government. Besides, liberating booty from a vanquished enemy was a time-honored tradition of the Arab.

Ali ibn el Hussein turned to stare at himself in a large oval mirror hung carefully from the wall over his massive, if untidy, desk. He was not a tall man, but he was physically quite powerful, due as much to his natural genetics as the rigorous workout program he adhered to daily. Fine, dark hair covered his head, parted neatly on the left side. His face was handsome in the cruel, Arab way, the black eyes overcast by equally black brows. His nose was lean, like a hawk's beak, the mouth a cruel cut of flesh from which hundreds of death sentences had been ordered in the course of his war-fed career. He wore the uniform of an Iraqi paratrooper, a simple pair of cloth jump wings sewn above one breast pocket. Around his waist was a well-oiled, brown stable belt, a Beretta .380 snugged into a custom holster of the same color. He carried a slim, stainless steel dagger beneath his smock. The soft leather sheath was tucked between his T-shirt and the tight-fitting upper portion of his pants. Standard jump boots were laced around his feet and ankles. Their shine was marred by the last several days' constant movement from command center to command center.

Wasn't it the American general, Sherman, who'd said war was hell? Hussein rubbed his hands on his pants as yet another artillery round impacted somewhere within the city limits. Before leaving he had a great deal of work to accomplish, beginning with the killing of those political prisoners still under his authority. Then there was the destruction of the water desalinization plants, the final order to blow up the oil wells nearest the city, and the transfer of hundreds of Kuwaiti citizens north into Iraq. These would be traveling with the army convoys attempting to break out of the city. Colonel Hussein hoped the Americans would refuse to bomb the long lines of trucks and armor if it was known there were hostages aboard.

The colonel released his image by walking away from the mirror's now-empty pool. Scattered field reports put American and French armor deep within southern Iraq, where they were engaging the Republican Guard units dug in across the border. The highway to Basra offered little assurance of getting home alive, because the air had been controlled by coalition forces since the beginning of the war. The sea, also, provided little hope of escape. American battle groups sailed through the Gulf with impunity, dropping off coastal raiding parties at will and sinking the pitiful naval units Iraq still could send to sea. Ali knew he would simply have to take his chances and run the gauntlet, leaving at nightfall and traveling with shrouded lights as fast as the littered highway would allow. His goal was simply to get far enough over the border to turn toward Umm Qasr, a tiny town on the coast. He'd ordered several fully equipped Land Rovers to be stashed away at a friend's home, just in case the fortunes of war went against his cousin's scheming.

Better safe than sorry, as the godless ones said.

"Colonel? You wished to see me?" Captain Ibrahim of the Republican Guard stood warily in the door, a shouldered AK-74 assault rifle clearly in view.

Hussein motioned the officer in. "Captain, anything new as to the battle for the city?" The senior officer pulled up a once-lavish but now soiled chair and sat, indicating that the younger man might do the same.

Ibrahim remained standing, his hand sliding down the blued barrel of the AK, coming to rest atop its shrouded front sight. "The Resistance is attacking our roadblocks and observation posts in the southern sectors with great success. The new airport is under siege, and the northern portion of the city is experiencing house-to-house fighting with members of the Kuwaiti Special Forces, who apparently have been infiltrating the capital for several days now.

"We continue to hold the coast, but to what purpose I cannot tell. It is now obvious the American Marines will not land against us as first thought, a good joke on us, yes?"

Hussein swatted a fly which was attempting to land on his battle tunic. "No, not a good joke, Captain. We've tied up several divisions protecting their approach from the sea, units which could be better used elsewhere. Make sure we concentrate our forces where they can bottle up the insurgents until at least tonight. I want a clear lane when the staff makes its departure for Iraq."

The grim and tired officer nodded. "About the prisoners . . ."

"Shoot them," ordered the colonel. "Better yet, take them downstairs into the basement and rig the building with explosives. That way we will bury them as well as remove them from the face of the earth. I depart at 1600 hours, so set your charges to blow anytime after 1615. Questions?"

"Am I then free to take my men and escape?"

Ali ibn el Hussein laughed. The sound was startling, given the circumstances, and the captain took a step back as his commander enjoyed what had to be a private joke to which only he possessed the punch line. "Escape?" mused Hussein. "I think the term 'flee' is more appropriate, my good captain. Yes, take your men and head for the border as soon as the building collapses.

"I would suggest traveling on isolated roads. Perhaps those nearest the coast would be best. The coalition against us will no doubt target the main arteries, and I expect to see American and Saudi tanks on the horizon any time.

"If you break out then fight your way to Baghdad. Come to what is left of the palace and ask for me by name. I shall see that you are taken care of. On this you have my word."

Ibrahim nodded absently, motioning toward the empty chair offered earlier. Hussein stretched out a hand; the invitation to sit was still open. Unslinging his rifle, the Republican Guard officer finally sat. The depth of the chair surprised him as he settled into it. After a moment, he spoke. "And what of Iraq, Colonel? The television seems to tell us our homeland is shaken to its core by the American air attacks. What faces us upon our return?"

The two men sat in silence as gunfire punctuated the afternoon heat. Tanks could be heard rumbling past the command center, their heavy treads grinding over shards of broken glass and abandoned equipment. Somewhere down the hall a television was on; CNN reports were still coming in as Kuwait City became the prize of those rushing madly across the desert in search of a final victory. Saddam Hussein had gambled and lost, misreading the signals sent by the American ambassador, miscalculating the world's reaction to his grab for greater power and influence in the Middle East.

Colonel Hussein pursed his lips, wetting them with a pink tongue before speaking. "Captain Ibrahim, the world as a whole knows little of Iraq and its fight for survival. Seven times in history we have been conquered. The Persians, Greeks, Romans, Arab, Mongol, Ottoman, and lastly the British. All have tied us with their yokes, but all have failed to enslave us as a people.

"Part of our problem lies in the lay of the land itself. Iraq is the hub of the wheel, open to the armies of Turkey, Iran, Saudi Arabia, Syria, Jordan, and Kuwait. We are the natural invasion route for our 'neighbors,' a route which brought the British to us in 1914, when they were afraid Germany might traverse us in order to assault India though Iran.

"Naturally, the discovery of our oil in 1923 entrenched the British rule, and the attempted coup of 1941 was squashed until the 'free officers' overthrew the king and kicked England out of Iraq for good. That was in 1958. Of course we didn't begin to exert our historic grip on the Middle East until Saddam came to power in 1968. The enormous rise in oil prices in the 1970s made us a nation to be treated with respect by the Western world. President Hussein used the income paid by the wasteful nations of Europe and the United States to build up a mighty army with which to protect Iraq from those who would see her on her knees again."

"It would appear that is precisely where we are today, Colonel," offered Ibrahim. "Will not the United States take advantage of the situation and move its armies into Baghdad itself?" The officer shifted the assault rifle so it lay across his dusty lap, absently slipping the safety on and off as he contemplated American tanks on the streets of his country's capital.

"No, I think this will not take place," consoled Hussein. "Bush has forged a fragile truce between the Arab countries, not out of their love for his countrymen, but out of their fear of us. At the same time there is no country in the region that wants to see the United States entrenched in Iraq. The perceived threat is too great to imagine.

"Remember our strategic position with respect to both Syria and Iran. The Syrians, who are our mortal enemies, could not bear having Israel on one frontier and America on the other. Iran also has learned the might of the United States when it comes to waging total war. A presence in Iraq under a government friendly to Bush would put a leash on any future plans Iran might have for dominating the Middle East."

" . . . and Russia?" interjected the captain.

"Ah, our 'allies' to the north. They definitely do not want the Americans holding such key territory. Bush would then effectively influence Israel, Saudi Arabia, Turkey, Egypt, Iraq, and the newly 'liberated' Kuwait.

"The Soviets could count only on Syria as an ally, but to what effect? Yemen, Ethiopia, and the Sudan are all disasters, devoid of political influence or value. Libya is as a man with no balls. Reagan's air attack on Qaddafi sent a strong message as to what awaits our friend if he should poke his head up out of the sands again. No, the Russians do not want Bush in Iraq, and they will stoke the Arab fires to ensure his forces stop short of a total victory."

Both men jumped up as a long burst of machine-gun fire echoed down the block outside Hussein's C&C center. Angry shouts erupted somewhere outside. Return fire from Ibrahim's guard unit started out slowly, then gained in intensity. "The Resistance," drawled the colonel. "We never did wipe them out to my satisfaction."

Ibrahim dug his forage cap out from a cargo pocket at his hip. "I need to return to my men and secure the area as you prepare to depart. The demolition specialists are already studying how best to bring this building down. It won't take but a few seconds once the charges are fired."

Hussein stepped to his desk and began cramming selected documents into a large aluminum briefcase. Most were files on interrogations carried out during the occupation. Some were personal papers he didn't want falling into the hands of the victors. Three truckloads of intelligence files had been sent to Basra; whether they had arrived safely the colonel did not know. As he rapidly scanned each folder for its worth to him, he issued the captain his last orders. "Make sure *all* the prisoners being held in the building are consumed by it. Once that is done, gather your men and fight your way north using the route we discussed. Before leaving, separate those of my staff who are with you from the others, and shoot them. Our enemies are talking of 'war crimes' and trials much like they conducted after Hitler's bid for power failed. I want as few potential witnesses available as possible, is that clear?"

The Republican Guard captain nodded his understanding. He was well aware of the death battalions which had kept order in occupied Kuwait, units whose mission was simply to shoot those who even talked of surrender or desertion. He himself had executed a number of faint-hearted Iraqi warriors in Kuwait City itself, leaving their corpses on the streets where the message was best seen, smelled, and therefore understood. "It shall be as you have ordered, Colonel." With that Ibrahim snapped a quick salute and left, the AK clenched by its wooden forestock, the safety off.

For a moment Hussein stopped his packing, staring at an imagined spot on the carpet beneath his booted feet. He would never dare voice his innermost thoughts about Saddam's insane move into Kuwait. To do so meant trusting someone, and his cousin's method of control made that inclination a death sentence. Stupid, he thought. Absolutely stupid of them to believe the United States wouldn't fight. Yes, Iraq needed more petrodollars than its oil fields could produce, that was a given. The eight years of war with Iran had drained the country's coffers as well as its will. With an economy falling apart at the seams it was difficult to watch the pompous asses of the al-Sabah family blatantly producing more oil than OPEC had agreed upon for each of its member nations. They produced more and sold it for less, making Iraqi oil a poor bargain on the world market. Saddam believed he could absorb the tiny country, claiming territorial rights dating back to 1961, when Kuwait was granted its independence from Britain. His cousin had moved then to take the newly freed country under Iraqi rule, but the English deployed their forces and Saddam backed down.

We are fools in the eyes of the world, raged the colonel. The once mighty war machine was being rapidly picked apart. Equipment purchased from the Soviets had proved to be no match for the wonder weapons manned by largely inexperienced American forces. Hussein harbored no doubts as to the relative ineffectiveness of the Arab allies, the Saudis perhaps the worst of all. Were the Americans, French, and British not on the front lines, the Arab coalition would falter and blow away. Only the Syrians were blooded. The rest were battered losers to Israel's tiny army and air force.

The metal container full, Hussein snapped its locks closed and set it heavily on the floor next to his desk.

Pulling his black beret from where it was hanging on a hook driven into the wall, he tugged the well-worn symbol of excellence onto his skull. The war outside of Iraq was nearly over, of that he was sure. It was the war to come, *inside* his country, that both concerned and excited him. Long a tribal country, Iraq was a simmering cauldron of bitter feuds and conflicts. On one hand there were the Shiite Moslems, whose primary supporters were based in Iran. A minority, the Shiites were constantly plotting against the government of Saddam Hussein. An idiot could foresee their using the war as an excuse to revolt in the southern portion of the country, where their numbers were the most concentrated.

To the north it would be those bastards the Kurds. The colonel hated them more than the Shiites, damned ignorant hill people who refused to face the fact that they represented only eighteen percent of the population of Iraq and therefore were owed nothing in terms of a homeland, which the misfits constantly were going to war over. Sunni Moslems, the Kurds possessed their own language and culture, and were as much a pain in the ass to the Turks and Iranians as they were to Saddam Hussein. They had rebelled during the war with Iran, supplied primarily by the Russians and Iranians, and they would no doubt do so now that Iraq was reeling from the punches the world had thrown it. *If* his cousin could maintain his grip on the reins of power they would be fighting Shiites in the south and Kurdish rebels to the north. It was a logical conclusion as far as the colonel was concerned. You simply had to understand Iraq's history to know it would happen.

It was nearing time to go. A last look at the office which had been his home for seven months, then he was out the door and heading down the long hall to where his paratroopers awaited him. The fight in the south would be hard but short, he considered, as his boots slapped against the hard tile floor. Basra would be the key, but the Shiites were poorly organized and not even Iran would be bold enough to supply overt aid to the rebels. The north would be a longer war. The mountains were difficult to secure

and the Kurds would be on their home turf. They could
be beaten, of this Hussein was sure. But it would be a
conventional ground battle, because the United States had
destroyed Iraq's ability to wage an air campaign.

"We're ready," spoke a gruff-looking Iraqi NCO. The
man was caked in concrete dust, and his assault rifle was
scarred with scratches and dents from the fighting he'd
taken part in since entering Kuwait by air. "I've assembled
only the best fighters, the most loyal. If ever there was a
chance to get back across the border, Colonel, it is with
those here today."

Captain Tarik Ibrahim watched the three-vehicle forma-
tion leave, its occupants now committed to a race against
time and nearly certain death. The battle-hardened Iraqi
understood his colonel's need to escape the oncoming
forces of the coalition. The spectacle of Kuwait City was
enough to warrant his hanging by the neck until dead.
Of course there would be little crying for the dead and
displaced in Baghdad, reasoned the captain. The victors
were always excused their atrocities. The vanquished were
held accountable simply because they'd been unfortunate
enough to lose.

Spinning on his heels, Ibrahim gestured for his demo
men to get on with it. Inside he could already hear
his guardsmen shoving the protesting prisoners down
the emergency stairwells. Screams and muted grunts
exploded from the building's innards as boots and gun
butts struck pitiful flesh. In all there were roughly 150
captives, all arrested from the local population. Some
were bona fide Resistance fighters. Others were simply
hostages taken in an attempt to stall Resistance attacks
on Iraqi military personnel. A few were criminals—rapists
and murderers, mostly. There was a smattering of Iraqi
turncoats and deserters, and a black marketeer or two.
Scum, all of them.

Ibrahim stepped into the foyer of the command center. Soldiers were bustling about, some of them carrying
sealed boxes of documents, others busily taking anything

not nailed down or claimed by another soldier as his own. Remembering the colonel's order concerning the disposable members of his staff, the captain had already sequestered them on the second floor. When asked what would become of them he'd answered that a number of armored vehicles were en route to whisk them to safety. This had satisfied the overfed fools, many of the three-dozen or so staff rats simply finding a clear spot on the floor to catch a quick catnap on until the imaginary trucks arrived.

It would be as much fun blowing the building up around those camel turds as it would be dropping their dead asses and one hundred tons of concrete and furniture on the malcontents in the basement, concluded the Republican Guard commando. Ibrahim was a field soldier who'd fought the Iranians for four long years before preparing for the invasion of Kuwait. He held rear-echelon troops in low regard; their jobs were necessary, but far too soft for his liking. Yes, he would get quite the thrill out of spilling their blood at the order of his commander.

"Captain! We are prepared to fire the charges at your will."

"Excellent," replied the officer. "You are sure the entire structure will be destroyed completely?"

"Sir, I am positive of my skill with explosives. Did I not meet your expectations with the destruction of the power plant?"

Ibrahim clapped the disgruntled demo man on the back. They'd been together through the entire campaign and no better powder monkey existed as far as the captain was concerned. "Your skill is beyond reproach, Sergeant. If you tell me the building is ready to fall, I believe you."

"Clear the area!" ordered the sergeant. In a rapid but orderly fashion the guardsmen began flowing from the building, running across the street to take up defensive positions from which to escape the coming avalanche of steel girders and poured concrete. Gunfire was now heard coming from several blocks up the wide boulevard, causing worried looks to cross the soldiers' faces as they darted at a crouch across open spaces unprotected by their comrades' firepower.

"The prisoners?" asked Ibrahim.

"Some were killed in the hallways as we moved them. Others 'fell' in the stairwells and never got up again. Most are happily tucked away in the basement, chanting their prayers and looking for a way out we might have missed." The Iraqi corporal blew a long string of snot from his nose into the gutter, a crooked smile on his face as he wiped the drippings from his lush mustache.

Ignoring the glob of mucus near the toe of his boot, the captain only nodded. "Let's blow it and be gone," he ordered. "Someone is getting too close for my liking. I'll be damned if I'm going to fight tanks with my bare hands at this stage of the game. The colonel is well on his way, if Allah wills it so. Find the sergeant and give him my blessing."

"And the colonel's staff?" questioned the junior noncom.

"God is great," retorted Ibrahim.

Grinning, the man scampered away.

Taking cover in a well-fortified bunker less than a hundred yards from the doomed building, the captain greeted those around him with a wink. The sudden explosion caused him to drop his head in reflex. The rumbling sound of over-stressed beams and walls rolled across the silent men like a heavy wave of sea water. A single scream rose up from the heaving edifice, its wail one of disbelief and abject betrayal. Then it was gone, wiped away, as tons of ruptured building materials collapsed on top of all those trapped inside.

When it was over only a thick pall of choking dust was left to remind the captain of his latest accomplishment. "Assemble and report," he ordered. "We need to get moving or face fighting the Americans within the hour." His warning had its desired effect. Two platoons of guardsmen hurriedly assembled, their weapons at the ready.

"Captain! The men are accounted for except for three. Shall we search for them?"

Ibrahim shook his head. "No. We head for the frontier now. Few of us will survive this last battle, have no illusions about that. Our mission for Iraq is accomplished. We have destroyed their wicked city and soft life-style. The riches they once taunted us with are now ours to enjoy. Their men lie buried in the sand. Their women mourn for the demise of their country. No one doubts the strength and will of the Iraqi army this day!"

Their grins told him they knew he was full of shit, and his own self-conscious smile confirmed their hunch. Iraqi had gotten its ass kicked and kicked good. First the stalemate of the war with Iran, and now the calamity of Kuwait. There was nothing left to do but kill as many of the enemy as possible while hotfooting it toward Baghdad. Ibrahim waved his arm forward. The long march home was about to begin.

# CHAPTER

## 3

Thornton turned at the sound of Frank Hartung entering their cramped quarters aboard the *Curtis* and noted with satisfaction the steaming cup of coffee being handed him by the retired sergeant-major.

"Thought you'd be ready for a cup," exclaimed Frank.

"Roger that, and thanks. How's the rest of the team?"

Propping his feet up the veteran of more than a number of wars in the shadows politely toasted his comrade-in-arms with a cup of his own. "They're showering, shaving, and shitting, all in that order. Rowe's hot for a sitrep on the air strike. We should have photos from our eye-in-the-sky shortly."

Bo brought the heavy ceramic cup to his lips and sipped gently at the coal-black liquid it held. The trip back to the *Curtis* had been uneventful, the burning Zodiac base a funeral pyre which lit the night for miles around. The SEALs were still working inland and were not expected back until the next morning. From all accounts the ground war was progressing smoothly. Saddam's forces were being hammered at every turn. "Nice to have a war we're winning, isn't it?"

Hartung laughed. "Yeah, isn't it though. Lot of lessons learned since Vietnam, and not all of them having to do with tactics."

"Letter from Lin says the entire country is supporting the troops like crazy. Got yellow ribbons up, flags, the whole nine yards. Guess the antiwar assholes haven't been too successful this time around."

Frank Hartung grimaced at the memory of the Vietnam protestors, a bitter taste in his mouth which wasn't due to the coffee. "There's a group which didn't learn a damn thing from history, and I'm delighted to hear they're taking a beating in the streets over this.

"The American people as a whole have figured out that the troops and the politics of a conflict are two separate parties. Especially with the volunteer army and a situation where Hussein is obviously someone we can't tolerate as a world figure. I still haven't heard old Hanoi Jane speak out against our presence here, and Abbie-baby showed his colors by checking himself out of the network early. It's one thing to want peace—and every soldier I know does—but another to demand it at any cost."

Thornton pulled a dry black T-shirt over his well-muscled torso. A steady diet of exercise kept him in superb physical shape. Each workout ended with a three-mile run along the beach when he was at home. Aboard ship there was a small gym, which most of the commandos used on nearly a twenty-four-hour basis, with runs around the deck taking care of the aerobic side of the house. "Gotta be a bunch of old hippies coming out of the woodwork for one last fling, plus the hanger-ons who think they know what's going down but actually haven't the foggiest. We're making history out here, Frank. Bush is playing it right down the line and once it's over we'll be back home within a month. The antiwar folks are gonna look stupid and they're gonna disappear as soon as the dust settles. Most will find something else to bitch about. They're the kind of people for whom any cause will do as long as there's a camera around to record it."

Hartung agreed. "It's a great country, Bo. No one said it was going to be easy, and sure as shit no one said it was going to be perfect. You and I have seen the world, and we know what a shithole it can be. America has its problems, always has and always will. But, when it comes right down to it we're a pretty damn good people for the most part. The troops are coming home winners this time around, and maybe it'll rub off on all the other poor sons-of-bitches who fought in the jungles of Southeast Asia and Central America too."

Dropping onto his cramped bunk Thornton stretched out. It felt good to relax. The rolling of the ship was comforting as they plowed through the Gulf. He was safe here, safe and secure with his friends. Without thinking he reached for the Browning, whose butt was sticking up out of its holster on his combat harness. He left it on second thought, as he noticed Frank watching him. "Old habits die hard, eh, you old bastard."

"It ain't like it used to be, but it'll do," responded Hartung. "Calvin says we're in for the long haul on this, but there's something brewing at the White House with our name on it. Seems the President wants to make an example out of someone in the Iraqi military *if* we don't get Saddam himself. They're holding off alerting us, but you can bet it'll be soon given the pace of operations."

"Frank," asked Bo, "do you think we'll go all the way into Baghdad?"

The Special Ops soldier sipped absently at his coffee for a moment before answering. "We said we'd only liberate Kuwait, not Iraq. Regional politics will demand we hold to that even though all reasoning says we ought to bring that butcher down hard. Another major concern has to do with who'd replace the bastard. If the Shiites grab control the country will become an extension of Iran's political goals. The Kurds are only interested in a piece of land of their own, and the communists are too few and too ineffectual to be considered at all.

"As far as I know there's no one man or party our government has cultivated enough so that a replacement government would work in our favor, which is what it is all about regardless of what the world's dreamers would have us believe. So I kinda got it figured that we'll leave it to the Iraqi people to get Hussein out of power, and if they fail it'll be such a disaster that he'll spend years digging the country out of the rubble."

"Nice scenario, Sergeant-Major. How about democracy in Kuwait while you're at it?"

"Fuck that noise!" Frank coughed, setting the empty cup on the deck. "The Saudi government won't stand for it because they know such a revolution in thought would roll over the border into their backyard within months. The al-Sabah family isn't interested in granting the kinds of freedoms we have back home, and they don't have to. Oh, we might see women get to vote, but only Kuwaiti women. Not much of an effect in whatever election they might have back on the block . . . once the block's been rebuilt, that is.

"Fact of the matter is this. Kuwait's been wasted and it'll take years to put the puzzle back together. Folks back home will lose interest in how the political machine is being run within six months, after all, we got our own problems, right? The focal point will shift back to Israel and some kind of peace with its neighbors, which old George is already working on if I have him pegged right. Besides, we ain't fighting for democracy and you and I both know it."

"What for then, Frank? Somehow I thought there was some apple pie in there somewhere."

"Shiittt, dream on, brother. Kuwait isn't only oil, it's investments as well. There's been so much money pumped into Kuwait that the returns alone equal eighty-five percent of what the oil pumped out does. There are damn few Kuwaitis who 'work' for a living, with mostly foreigners doing all the shit details while the citizens cruise around in their BMWs. Not a bad deal if you're holding a Kuwaiti passport.

"Now if that dumb shit in Baghdad had played his cards right he might have waltzed into the Emir's palace with nary a shot fired. But by using the iron fist rather than the velvet glove he pissed off everybody who had anything in-country. Not only is he upsetting the golden apple cart, he's scaring the shit outta his neighbors, primarily Saudi Arabia. Too much money talking now, Bo. So we're fighting for good old capitalism which is the basis of America, like it or not."

Thornton's eyes were closed. His breathing deepened as the tide of sleep overcame him. The tension of the mission was ebbing out of his pores like slow sweat. Frank's voice was lulling him downward into a bottomless sleep, but the truth of what he was saying registered even as Thornton slipped away from the reality of his surroundings.

Frank Hartung watched the man who was his best friend sleep. With a smile he carefully made his way out of the tiny cabin they shared, figuring he should check in on the others anyhow. It was good that Bo was getting some well-deserved shut-eye. From all accounts it had been a heck of a mission.

"Thornton, you awake? It's me, Raven. We got major problems on the perimeter. The captain asked me to have you come up and take a look." Sergeant First Class Jerry Raven flicked the tiny flashlight off as Bo sat up. The pungent smell of El Salvador reminded him of where he was even as he reached for his boots. San Miguel was deep inside "Indian country," the base a launch point for Army operations into the department of Morazan, which seemed to grow guerrillas like corn these days. He'd flown in from Panama a week before, directed by his battalion commander to visit with the 3/7th teams in the field. Raven's bunch had been in-country for three months now, and by all accounts they were doing a hell of a job for Colonel Monterrosa.

Grabbing a borrowed M16 Thornton shrugged into his LBE, the Colt .45 automatic safely tucked into its GI-issue holster at his hip. American policy in El Salvador was murky when it came to the fifty-five advisors operating with the host country's military. Most of the guys carried serious firepower now. The threat of guerrilla attack was increasing as the war escalated. Bo knew of two earned Purple Hearts already, as well as a Silver Star which had been taken back and downgraded when some political asshole in Washington started whining about the good citizens of America finding out their boys down south were involved in more than just a "police action."

The night was cool with just a touch of moisture in the air as he made his way across the compound to where Raven and the rest of the team was gathered. "What's shakin', Captain? Got dinks in the wire or deserters heading home to Momma?"

"Looks like a probing action, Bo. We've had a Starlight scope on two little bastards snipping wire just outside our sector of the perimeter for about fifteen minutes now. No traffic has come by for over an hour, which is odd on a Friday night. If I wasn't such an optimist I'd say we're fixing to get hit, and sometime soon."

Thornton nodded. "The commandant release half the troops for party-time like he promised?"

Raven spoke. "Sure as shit did. Everyone in town knew the *quartel* was going to be half-manned, and we got one company out on an operation to boot. The captain couldn't convince the dumb bastard to hold off until tomorrow night when they'd be back in. Seems he wanted to look good in front of the troops, especially with Monterrosa's popularity rating down among the ranks."

Thornton climbed the spindly wooden ladder which led to the roof of the team's CP. A thick wall of sandbags ran its entire length, three .30 caliber Browning machine guns mounted on tripods to cover the corner of the *quartel* given them by the base commander. The team had found the old guns in the arms room gathering rust, and it had taken seven of the weapons to make three which were operational. There was plenty of ammunition, and Raven had himself supervised the building of the gun platform so they could best cover the wide open fields leading up to the *quartel*'s gates. Bo was impressed by the young NCO's knowledge of his job. "Gimmie the scope and let's see what our visitors are up to, shall we?"

Lifting the awkward NVG to his eye Thornton adjusted the focus, scanning the barbed-wire perimeter slowly until he came to rest on the two intruders. With a start he realized there was a large group of men crawling up behind the dynamic duo, all armed and obviously not members of the home team. "Better get behind the guns and send a runner to the TOC," he hissed between grim lips. "The party's about to start . . ."

A sharp percussion heralded the *whoooosh* of an inbound rocket as a guerrilla unloaded on the compound with an RPG-7. The team threw themselves as one onto the hard roof even as the missile exploded against the *quartel's* steel gates, causing them to buckle under its fiery impact. With a rush the first assault group scrambled through the cut wire, firing their assault rifles and machine guns on the run. Bullets poured into the startled Salvadoran compound, and three soldiers died outright as fragments from a second rocket caught them in the open.

Bo rolled in behind one of the .30's. Raven was right beside him as they slapped a long chain of ammunition into the feed tray. Cocking the heavy weapon with a vicious jerk of the charging handle to the rear, Thornton called for someone to put a flare up so he could begin dealing out a little payback of their own. With a loud *pop!* the parachute flare leaped skyward, roaring overhead where it exploded and began to burn brightly. As the white parachute drifted slowly downward, the flare's illumination revealed they were under attack by at least a company's worth of FMLN "freedom" fighters.

"Shit oh me," whispered Raven as he began feeding the linked rounds into the now-firing Browning. "I do believe we're now involved in a combat operation. The embassy ain't gonna like hearing about this one . . ."

Thornton caught the lead element of a group splitting off toward their section of the wall in a firestorm of hot steel pellets. The two other machine guns were working now, their snouts spitting serious lead downrange. Bodies jerked and bumped like deranged bowling pins as the massive copper jackets collided with muscle, bone, and meat. "Watch the barrel . . . watch the freaking barrel!" he yelled at Raven.

"She's heating up, but no problem!" screamed the assistant gunner. "Keep the bursts short and we'll be fine!"

A thick cloud of cordite was beginning to choke those on the brass-littered rooftop. An RPG roared overhead as its gunner attempted to zero in on the stubborn blockhouse. The round exploded on the other side of the *quartel*, where several families were living. Thornton could see more figures running across the fields toward the compound. The roar of gunfire was overwhelming, making communication impossible except by hand-and-arm signals and quick glances. Raven was pouring a can of motor oil over the .30's vented barrel, cooling it somewhat as Bo's bursts became longer and more pronounced. The other AGs were doing the same. The fear of burning out the rifled barrels was a real one, despite the increasing need to maintain a carpet of fire on the advancing enemy soldiers.

From behind came the heavy *thump* of one of the camp's mortars. Two Green Berets manning the tube dumped illumination rounds down its throat as quickly as possible. The night began to brighten as the results of their efforts exploded high above the countryside, and the team began to alternate high explosive with illumination rounds in an effort to cut the guerrillas off from their preplanned avenues of advance. "That's Cerillo and Kenny," yelled Raven into Bo's ear. "Best mortar men in the battalion!"

Thornton kept the Browning's trigger depressed. The vintage weapon was singing now. Raven poured more oil across the barrel as Bo fed the tray with one hand, traversed the gun with the other, and fed a steady stream of man-killers into the killing ground to his front. A dull *thud!* announced a grenade of some sort going off at the base of the protective wall below them. Smoke and splinters of plaster shot straight upward and showered the defenders with debris. Bo had no idea how the fight was going elsewhere. The team was essentially cut off from the rest of the compound as the battle's ferocity grew.

"I got through to the embassy!" yelled Captain Travers as he flopped down beside Thornton, M-16 in hand. "Advised them we were under heavy attack and requested support. Ain't nothing available from the air force as they're flying support against a G base camp in Usulutan!"

"Can't they divert a jet or two our way?" barked Thornton. Usulutan wasn't that far off and certainly a trapped A-team was priority given the political climate of the war.

"Don't count on it," said Travers. "MilGrp commander says to hang on as long as we can. If it looks like the base is going to be overrun we're to boogie on the E&E plan!"

"Where?" shouted Bo. "Damned guerrillas are all over the joint! This is a major push, boss! Figure the FMLN to hit us when half the camp's away and Monterrosa is operating elsewhere. We'd be lucky to get a hundred meters without taking hits!"

Travers raised himself up on his elbows, levering the M-16 over the sandbagged barrier so he could burn a magazine off at the flitting figures trying once again to close with them. "So much for aimed fire," he spat while changing magazines.

"Gotta gun down!" Thornton turned to watch the crew on his right flank angrily tearing away at a wounded Browning. "Get one of the sixties from the downstairs!" ordered Bo. There were two of the LMGs tucked away in the team's living area, cleaned and oiled from a range they'd been on the day before.

Travers slipped in between Raven and the smoking .30 caliber cannon. "Go! Get the damned pig up here and take the right flank! I'll AG for Thornton . . . see if we can get some 203 rounds downrange too!" With a nod of understanding the sergeant slipped rapidly rearward on his belly. Hot brass burned the palms of his hands and exposed stomach as his T-shirt was pulled free.

At least one other mortar was now coughing away, this one manned by a Salvadoran crew trained by the team earlier on. Rounds were impacting nicely in the fields. Geysers of rich earth erupted with every explosion. Thornton heard the M-60 start up as Raven ran his first, fast belt through the system. Red tracers licking outward as the Special Forces operator began arcing the barrel into the faltering ranks of the guerrillas. On Bo's left flank the Browning crew had run out of oil and were pissing into empty ammo cans. The putrid smell of burning piss stung at Thornton's nose as the can was poured along the top of the barrel. Out front the Gs were beginning to fall back. The furious onslaught of triple-gun fire provided by the A-team had been an unexpected factor in their attack equation.

"I think we've got them on the run!" wheezed Travers as he broke open another can of .30 caliber link. "No more rockets either!"

Bo nodded. His face was stained black by the burned cordite of the thousands of rounds he'd fired. Thick, salty rivers of sweat were pouring down his temples and cheeks, gathering in a pool at the base of his skull, then proceeding to soak the upper portion of his broad back. His hands were numb from the gun's steady vibration, and the fingers of his left hand were cut and swollen from the jerking of the sharp steel links running over them as he'd fed the chamber. The small of his back was cramped, and his legs likewise affected from the tension of the moment. The even cadence of a 203 grenade launcher came to him, the disabled Browning's crew having abandoned the weapon and taken up their small arms to support the remaining guns on the roof. Between the mortars and 203's they were beginning to tear the enemy up. Only a meager attempt at supporting fire coming from far out in the darkness where FMLN gunners were laid up.

"Embassy on the horn, sir!"

Travers nodded. "Can you work this thing without me?"

Thornton choked an affirmative out of his dry mouth. With that the captain was gone, clambering down the ladder and rushing into the team room where the SatCom radio was housed. Bo grabbed the last can of ammo left for the gun, popping the metal top up and jerking the first linked round out. His body was half-buried in spent brass. A sheen of burned oil coated everything around where he lay. The smell of fried piss was still trapped in his nostrils, and his head was beginning to pound from the heavy resonance of the combined weaponry going off.

"Link it and chamber!" shouted Raven from somewhere off his left flank. "We got a group of the bastards pinned down at your ten o'clock!"

Obediently Bo flipped the feed cover upward, raking the last trio of spent links clear of the gun, then laying the blunt-nosed bullet on track. Squeezing the cover down until he heard it *click* into position, he then charged the handle and traversed the smoking, steaming barrel on target. Raven's gun was already picking the huddled mass of confused soldiers apart, and the pounding yammer of the .30 was ripping what was left to shreds as Thornton brought the beast to bear. It was over within seconds. Nothing but smoking earth and blood-soaked clothing was left to view.

"We got people in the camp!" screamed one of the 203 gunners, his M-16 spitting rounds at a band of invaders who'd breeched the wall near the cook shed and were now tossing grenades and prepared charges into any open door or window they could find.

"Fuck!" roared Bo. Leaving the Browning he rolled backward, catching up his rifle and taking aim at a running figure headed their way. Snapping the trigger back, he dropped the man with a single shot, shooting him again as he attempted to push himself up off the ground. Raven turned the M-60 inward, tracking on two men who were half-hidden behind the *quartel* commander's brand new Land Rover. "Crank it out!" ordered Thornton.

With a grin that split the smudged features of his face the Special Forces gunner began ripping the vehicle apart. Long streams of 7.62 lead pounded the Rover into pulp, blasting glass free and zippering molded metal to shreds. The Gs made a break from cover, and the team's combined firepower knocked them off their feet as well over two hundred rounds were sucked into their flesh. "Sorry about the colonel's rig!" offered Raven as he recharged the smoking gun in his hands.

"He'll get over it," laughed Bo.

Sunrise revealed the bodies of those left behind, their mangled and bloodied remains strewn around the *quartel* in postures of violent death. Deep craters pockmarked the team's free-fire zone. The mortars and rifle-launched grenades had torn the ground apart like high-powered fists of fury. The sweet smell of decaying tissue was making itself known. It would be replaced soon enough with the powerful aroma of rot unless the bodies and their severed parts were swiftly policed up and buried. Thornton, standing on the roof amid the refuse of the night's battle, surveyed the scene quietly and alone. His memory recognized the information his eyes were sending to the brain. Vietnam had been like this on several occasions. Build a camp and expect it to get hit, that was a rule. They'd been fortunate to have driven off the attackers with minimal losses of their own, although some soldiers in town on leave had been rounded up by the Gs and shot while the attack was in progress.

Travers climbed wearily up the ladder, pulling himself onto the roof with an audible sigh. Carefully stepping between the silent Brownings he brushed a layer of powder-smudged brass off the sandbagged wall and sat. "MilGrp commander is on his way, got the SOUTHCOM commander with him as well. Should arrive in about ten minutes, so we've got to have our shit together about all of this."

Bo chuckled to himself. "You know as well as I do they'll shake our hands and then tell us it never happened. Damned rules say we can't be involved in combat even when it's forced upon us. There won't be any CIBs coming out of this war, Captain."

The young officer nodded in agreement. The Combat Infantryman's Badge was highly regarded by those in the field of combat arms. It said you'd been there and it told the world your actions had been honorable. Every grunt worth his salt looked forward to the opportunity to earn a CIB. The successful attack on Grenada had whetted the appetite of everyone serving in El Salvador. "In Special

Forces we do the job regardless of whether official credit is given or not. My team earned the right last night. Shit, the *quartel* might have been taken if they hadn't been here with all the right stuff. But you're right about the CIBs, Thornton. We'll never see 'em. That's the politics of it all."

Bo squeezed the officer's shoulder in understanding. He'd fought well, taking all the chances his men did and keeping his calm when they looked for leadership. Yeah, the kid had kept it together in a big way for his first time under fire. Better than Bo'd expected he might. "Those that count will know, believe me. The general can wish it away, the embassy can hope the media never finds out, and the rest of the army can pretend this kind of shit never happens unless the action is 'declared.' But we know, and the Gs know, and between the two of us it ain't hard to figure out who came out the better man."

Travers managed a weak laugh. "Roger that, Bo. We had a team take incoming several months back to the west of us. They sent some back of their own and called in a gunship. The Sals tried to award them Salvadoran CIBs, but the embassy put a stop to that little ceremony most ric-tic. I guess we just hang in there and drive on with the mission, eh?"

"Yes, sir. That's what it's all about. Someday they'll retrograde everything and proper credit will be given. History is a funny thing. Sooner or later the truth comes out and everyone wonders why it was such a big deal to begin with. Anyhow, we're due a major conflict soon. Been too much going down around the world for us not to have to pull a little rank somewhere. You'll get your chance, count on it."

The distant drone of incoming choppers brought both men's eyes to the sky. "Pony show time. Here comes the brass to find out just how much they need to say if questions are asked. I'll get the team together, make sure they've got the right hats on. Don't need to take a bitching over *that* issue!" Travers shimmied down the ladder and began barking orders to Raven and the team.

All of them were washed up and shaven, noted Bo.

*Stupid way to run a war,* he said to himself as the first bird touched down. But the geopolitics of the region were confused at best, with Nicaragua devouring itself and Panama's dictator shaking his ass at Uncle Sam every time you turned around. It took a special kind of soldier to do what Travers's team had done, and Thornton knew they'd be back on the range tomorrow, teaching mortars or machine guns and loving it. They were just that way.

"Bo! You want to go out and meet the general with us?" Raven stood patiently, his pistol belt buckled and what looked like a fresh coat of boot polish glistening in the sun's rays.

"Yeah, might as well. I know both those assholes personally, so it'll be fun watching them squirm as they give you guys the 'this shit never happened' routine. Save me a seat on the jeep, I'm on my way down."

The beat-up vehicle bumped its way around holes and body parts, and its occupants watched as squads of Salvadoran soldiers continued cleaning up the battlefield. Monterrosa himself was coming in later, having been briefed on the attack on the *quartel* by radio that morning. Bo noted that all three choppers were on the ground now, their blades spinning loudly as knots of men dashed out from beneath them, coming up short as they recognized the extent of the battle. *Thank the Lord we didn't lose anyone last night,* thought Bo to himself. You can hide a lot of things, but a body is pretty tough, although it could be done. Shit, enough dead Green Berets were left in Southeast Asia over borders where they weren't supposed to be.

Some things never changed, mused Thornton. Some things never change.

# CHAPTER
## 4

"Rise and shine, Bo. Cal needs us in the briefing room." Mike Bannion shook the sleeping man a few more times, noting with satisfaction that his team leader was finally getting some well-deserved rest. As Thornton stirred, Bannion raised himself to his full height and stretched. The former SLAM agent was powerfully built as a result of brutal physical training from his days as a SEAL and DEA agent. A transfer from the Drug Enforcement Agency, where he'd been an operator in Southeast Asia, Bannion was now on the payroll of Springblade, or as they were now code-named, Camelot.

"What's shakin'?" asked Bo, swinging his feet over the bunk's rumpled lip. "Thought we were due some down time after last night's excursion."

Bannion shook his head. "Two things. First, we got a SEAL platoon jammed up and they need a reaction force ASAP. Got ambushed coming back down the river. They broke contact but have several wounded, and the raft's shot up too bad to travel.

"Second, Cal's been given a green light for a mission aimed at snatching some high-ranking Iraqi bozo for a war-crimes trial. Ground war's picked up pace, if you can believe that, and they're predicting a cease-fire anytime soon."

Thornton pulled his socks on, then shoved his feet into a dry pair of jungle boots. Speed-lacing them he asked

Mike to pull a lightweight wool sweater out of his open ruck. There was always a chill in the air, it seemed—strange considering they were supposed to be operating in the scorching hot desert.

"Ya look like a million bucks, boss," complimented Bannion.

"Wonderful," retorted Bo. "These SEALs under fire or we just gonna fly in and help load their gear?"

"Last contact said they were holed up a hundred meters inland from the river. No contact since the ambush, but they can't continue their float trip with the boat shot to shit like it is. We got a MH-47 standing by to fly us in. Shouldn't be too tough as they'll be a team of fast-movers off the *Midway* providing cover."

"Let's get it on," urged Thornton. "I know them boys are waitin' for a taxi and the Iraqis just might decide to follow up on one of their few successes."

"Hey, know why they don't have driver education classes and sex education in Iraq on the same day?" quipped Bannion as the two men strode down the narrow hallway toward a steep ladder leading topside.

"Why?" groaned Bo, taking the steps two at a time.

"The camels get too tired!"

"Why me, Lord?" asked Thornton out loud. "Why me?"

They went in heavily armed, carrying only what could be packed into their combat harnesses and uniform pockets. The mission was simple: locate the stranded SEAL platoon and bring them back to the *Curtis*. On board the sophisticated chopper known as the MH-47 were Thornton, Silver, Bannion, Rowe, and Frank Hartung, who claimed he'd been at sea so long he was beginning to think he was half fish. Also along for the flight were two Air Force pararescue men, or "PJs," as they were called.

The MH-47 was a sophisticated version of the MH-53, known in Vietnam as the "Super Jolly Green Giant." The Jolly Green possessed the power of a twenty-mule pack team and was used for resupply and troop movement missions. The Army employed it as an aircrew recovery vehicle, flying it in tandem with supporting gunships and fast-movers whenever a pilot was on the ground and in danger of being captured.

The rapid expansion of Special Operations demanded that an air asset be developed which could move teams into and out of denied areas without being detected. This meant a vehicle which was large enough to pack in two twelve-man teams plus their initial equipment and one which could operate in the worst terrain and weather.

The disaster of "Desert One," when the helicopter support proved to be the weak link in a daring but doomed plan to rescue American hostages being held in Iran, had given additional impetus to the development of the MH-47 system. Using the Jolly Green as a basis, researchers designed and tested a series of instrument packages which were then integrated into the chopper's airframe. The helicopter was then capable of inflight refueling, all-terrain navigation, and automatic hovering, thanks to a device called a "hover coupler."

What all this meant was that Thornton's crew was now zipping across the ocean's surface at over two hundred miles-per-hour, the pilots watching their Forward Looking Infrared sensor (FLIR) just in case a sand dune decided to pop up out of nowhere. Once over the SEALs, the recovery team would wait until the hover coupler was engaged, meaning once the aircraft was at the proper height and stability, Thornton & Company would fast-rope in. At that point they'd make contact while the Jolly Green ran a quick 360-degree racetrack before returning to extract their charges.

Sitting on the bare metal floor Bo rechecked his AK. He was pleased to see it hadn't gotten too banged up from the previous evening's trials. Bannion and Silver were carrying M-16's, Rowe a silenced H&K SVD, and Hartung a scoped M-14A1 just as a long shot. The PJs were content with their Colt Commandos, updated versions of the old CAR-15 Bo remembered from Vietnam. Each man's combat harness was fully loaded with everything from spare strobe lights and batteries to emergency medical gear. Just before they boarded the chopper they had been advised by Naval Intelligence that the SEALs were sitting tight, reporting no enemy activity or contact since they'd escaped the hasty ambush set for them.

"We're twelve mikes out," advised Hartung through his voice-activated mike. "Chopper's got commo with the knuckle-draggers. Everything still quiet."

Thornton nodded in the affirmative, touching each man on the team and flashing the jump master signal for "six minutes," the initial warning that it was time to get one's shit together. "Frank, we'll rope in and form a wagon wheel. I'll let the SEALs link up with us while you scout the area with the bird, copy?"

"Shit, and here I thought I was gonna get a chance to wiggle my old toes in the sand," groused Hartung.

"You'll get plenty of time for that if we go after Saddam's asshole cousin, you old goat! Right now I need you flying cover for us. Even as calm as everything sounds down there I don't want any surprises, dig?"

"Four minutes out," intoned the pilot as he cut in on the two men's conversation. "We've got a visual on an orange panel. That's your infil point, Mr. Thornton. Good luck!"

Bo pulled a pair of dark tanker's goggles down over his eyes. The rear ramp of the MH-47 was fully depressed now, the ground a blur as the chopper roared over it, altitude now one hundred feet AGL. Signaling to Bannion that they were about to infil, Bo watched the huge commando slip his right foot into the thickly coiled rope near the open cargo ramp. At Thornton's signal Mike would kick the rope clear of the ramp, a steel brace at eye level acting as an airborne anchor for the 150 feet of high strength line. Bo would leave the airframe first, forming a wide O with his boots around the rope, allowing them to act as a brake when he came close enough to touch down. His gloved hands were more guides than clamps. The weight of his body took him rapidly downward. An entire team could occupy ground within seconds using this improved method of the old fireman's pole, a considerable advance on clumsy rappel systems, which left men and aircraft dangerously exposed to ground fire.

"One minute!" yelled Hartung in Bo's ear.

The chopper suddenly flared, evening out and becoming rock-steady as the ground came into focus. Thornton could see the emergency panel for only a moment before it slipped underneath the airframe's gut. Glancing at Bannion, he gave the signal to kick. The rope flew outward and down. Each coil gracefully floated free until the line was fully deployed.

"Go!" roared Frank.

And Thornton went. Reaching forward so he was damn near off-balance, Bo grabbed hold of the rope up near its connecting point at the brace. Swinging strongly outward, he wrapped his feet around the thick braid, releasing some of the tension on his hands so that his weight began to respond to gravity's pull. In an instant he was gone, flying down the green umbilical cord as if shot from a cannon. Behind him Mike was already barreling downward, his booted heels scant inches above Bo's head. Like peas in a pod they descended onto the hard-packed desert floor. Hartung gave the crew chief a thumbs-up just as Silver touched down.

The powerful turbines began growling as the pilot gave the big chopper its head. The rope floated out behind the Jolly Green's ass like a tail on a kite. Sand was flying everywhere. Huge plumes of the fine grit swirled around the team. Their faces were buried in the crooks of their arms. Thornton knew the SEALs would be providing them cover until the storm settled, so he relaxed and just let the violent beating of the twin rotors flail away at him until the MH-47 was once again at altitude.

"So much for the nice hot shower," bitched Jason Silver as the Jolly Green slipped away from them at speed. "I got half of Iraq up my ass!"

"Better than down your throat," said Thornton, dusting himself off and adjusting his goggles. "Hey, here comes the welcoming party; look alive!"

Like wraiths the SEALs appeared in the distant haze of the day. They were dressed in the standard chocolate-chip desert camouflage uniforms of the American forces, their weapons held at the ready, their faces distorted by the sunglasses and goggles they wore to keep the blinding sun at bay. One of the men waved at Bo's group, and a broad smile-creased face as the two elements drew closer to each other. "If it ain't Mike Bannion," exclaimed the wry SEAL, once the two men were within arm's reach. "Thought you'd be chasing one of them swabbie-nurses on the *Curtis* around, my man."

"Hector, when I heard you'd fucked up your mission I just knew I'd have to leave all those sweet things alone just to save your dumb ass," laughed Mike. "How's your wounded? Okay?"

Hector Vejo nodded. "Some shrapnel in the face, one with a bullet up his butt. They're bitching like crazy, so you know they ain't hurtin' that bad. Fucking Iraqis got lucky and zapped us on the river. Maybe two squads of the pukes. Don't know if we counted any coup but they knew we weren't licked, and that ain't no shit!"

"You got a LZ picked out for the MH-47?" asked Thornton.

"Yeah, right next to our RON. The chopper can get in no sweat, it's all hard-pack just like this shit we're standing on. We already informed the bird. You wanna hump it on back and catch a lift?"

"You guys wanna know just how much sand I got up my ass?" complained Silver to the group. "Half of Iraq and a good portion of freaking Iran, that's how much!"

The group dissolved into laughter. Jason flipped them all the bird as they fell into single file and started for the SEAL's perimeter.

"Good mission?" asked Bo as he glided up next to Hector.

"Roger that. We located the pontoon bridges and painted them up real pretty. Air Force zapped them, one, two, three, and got half a dozen trucks in the process. It's a mess up around Basra, my man. Shit all over the place and firing going on in the city. I'd say we got a revolution or something taking place."

"Breaks my heart," said Thornton. "You see our piece of work on your way back down?"

"Fuck me, yes," chuckled the SEAL. "Old Wobbly turned that AO into black glass, believe me. Nothin' but scorched earth and bits of shit floating next to the shoreline. You guys marked that one to the T, a nice bit of work for a buncha old dudes."

Bo laughed at the left-handed compliment. "At least our boat didn't get itself shot to shit on the return trip. Guess that kind of experience comes with age, eh?"

"Touché!" exclaimed the Latin. "Buy ya beer once we're back on the *Curtis*."

Ten minutes later the men entered the waiting SEAL's perimeter. Rowe linked up with the Navy corpsman tending to the wounded, reporting to Thornton that they were both fit and eager to travel. Both Zodiacs were trashed. Two SEALs had cut their bottoms out to make them unusable if discovered. Silver was talking with the PAVE-LOW and Bannion was swapping lies with his former comrades as Hector supervised their preparations for extraction.

"Bo! Pilot says they got visual on a group of Iraqis waving white flags. He wants to know what we should do."

"Might be the same bastards that shot us up," growled Vejo. "I know what I'd *like* to do."

Thornton paused for a moment. "Jay, ask our boy how many there are. Maybe we can get some good intel outta this picnic if there's room enough to transport at least the ranking personnel."

Silver waved a hand in acknowledgment. "He says it's hard to say, maybe a dozen or more. What's the word?"

Bo turned to the SEAL team leader. "Your call, Hector. You got wounded and we got a full bird. Could be a trap for all I know."

Vejo looked around at his men. "We could at least check it out. Rope in a security team and make contact. One of my guys speaks the lingo real good. We ID the honchos, grab any documents they got, then promise to return in an hour."

" . . . and I won't come in your mouth," joked Bannion.

"Aye-aye," replied Vejo. "I don't mind losing two boats if I can bring back a POW. Kinda makes things even in front of the old man. Let's do it!"

Calvin Bailey listened in disbelief as the radiotelephone operator aboard the *Curtis* relayed the PAVE-LOW pilot's message. "Send Bo out for SEALs and he comes back with an Iraqi major, unfuckingbelievable!" The former DEA agent afforded himself a short laugh as the ship's bells began clanging. Men rushed to and fro as the *Curtis* prepared to receive her prisoners.

Taking his time he brushed past the hastily dressed Marines who were charging topside, their M-16s in hand. This was a good sign, reasoned Bailey. With what the President wanted from Bo this time around the unexpected success of a POW seemed to signal a positive beginning for the team's next mission. Of course this time they'd be heading deep into Iraq, looking for Colonel Ali Hussein, the "Butcher of Kuwait." Agency sources put him safely in Baghdad at his cousin's command bunker. A CNN video report had caught the colonel's features during one of the rare personal appearances old Saddam was making these days.

Yeah, leave it to Bo to take on what would be the toughest mission of the Special Ops war to date. Bush wanted at least one Hussein to pay for his crimes, and politically the colonel was just the ticket. Reaching his quarters, the former SEAL grabbed his combat harness off its steel peg and began checking it contents.

This time he'd be going in as well.

# CHAPTER

## 5

Conrad Billings remained seated as the meeting began breaking up. It was a beautiful day in Washington. The sky was clear and a hint of spring was tapping at the thick windowpanes evenly spaced along the far wall of the huge conference room. It had been a marathon session this morning, with the course of the war discussed at every turn. The Marines—God bless 'em—had raised the American flag above the U.S. Embassy in Kuwait City during the night, signaling the coming of the end for Saddam's army of looters and thugs.

"Conrad? How about a cup of coffee? I need to speak with you concerning your operators in the Gulf—if you have time, that is." Sam Kellerman was one of the President's primary movers and shakers when it came to those secret projects being carried out by Schwarzkopf's Central Command in Saudi Arabia. A dapper fellow with a quick sense of humor, Kellerman was pushing for some kind of war-crimes trial to be held in Kuwait once the fighting was over and Iraq defeated.

Billings lifted his half-full cup from the polished wooden table they'd been sitting at. "Your office or here, I'm free until 1500."

Kellerman looked around, seeming to consider whether he could talk openly in the nearly empty meeting area or if his nearby office might be more secure. The decision silently made, the man pulled out a chair and sat facing

Billings. "We're seventy-two hours into the ground phase and Saddam's 'supermen' are crawling out of the earth like rock chucks. Kuwait City is under attack from our Special Forces people and the Resistance, the 101st, First Division, Twenty-Fourth and French Sixth RDF are cutting the Republican Guard a new asshole in southern Iraq herself. Makes all the stalling and posturing worthwhile, given we're gonna kick Hussein's silly ass all over the Middle East."

Conrad poured both men full cups from an insulated pot. "You don't have to jerk me off, Sam. How heavily are we committed to this 'war crimes' deal, and is Saddam's bastard cousin still the primary target?"

Kellerman laughed, tipping his head in appreciation for Billings' directness. "Connie, the President is appalled by the destruction in Kuwait City. Colonel Hussein is responsible for over six hundred oil wells being set ablaze, not to mention the release of millions of gallons of oil into the Gulf when they thought we'd send the Marines ashore. Bad as all that is, the looting of the Kuwaiti banks, hospitals, museums, art galleries, stores, and every other source of spoils rivals Hitler's scourging of Europe.

"George is riding high on this thing. The Democrats fucked themselves royally by not backing his play during the Desert Shield phase, and now they're paying for it big-time. Old-fashioned patriotism is once again in vogue, the antiwar assholes about as popular as a leper at a massage parlor. We want to squeeze this thing for all it's worth, and that means bringing at least one bona fide war criminal to justice if at all possible."

"I smell politics seeping into this," cautioned Billings. "Are you saying we're not going to roll the tanks all the way into Baghdad? That's where the ultimate criminal is hiding out, or are we forgetting that?"

Kellerman sighed. "We tried to get Saddam with the Air Force but he's buried too deep. You might have heard rumors about a DELTA team going in to terminate the 'Mother of All Cocksuckers.' Well, that didn't work out too well either. The bottom line is that Saddam is probably going to live through this debacle, and that's a fact.

"Given my theory, we now have to consider the very real politics of the region once a cease-fire is declared. We *know* Saddam Hussein inside and out by now. Better yet, he knows *us* and he knows we're quite capable and willing to turn his lights off if he gets stupid again any time soon. If Hussein is removed from power, who takes over? No one we know about has the right stuff, and certainly we can't afford a proxy president supported by Iran or Syria.

"No, we keep old fuck-nuts in place and let him worry about rebuilding what's left of Iraq. Our fundamental goal was to liberate Kuwait, which is being accomplished. Parallel to that worthy notion was the destruction of Saddam's chemical and nuclear capabilities, two goals we've also seen realized. Right now General Schwarzkopf is paring down the man's oversized—and overrated, I might add—army. We're going to leave him just enough to maintain control in Iraq but not enough to bully his neighbors, which is why the northern and northeastern concentrations are being ignored for the time being."

Conrad took it all in without a trace of emotion on his face. The die was cast, that much was obvious. Saddam Hussein would be left in power despite the call for his people to rebel, an undertaking they couldn't help but fail at unless provided massive logistical and operational support by the United States. The Kurds were already staging raids and ambushes, actions which would bring down the untouched forces Kellerman had mentioned like God's own wrath. It would be a sharper fight in the south around Basra, simply because the Iraqi army would be fighting both the coalition forces and the Shiite rebels. But as long as U.S. forces held back it would be only a matter of time before Saddam would crush the spirited holy warriors, one by one. "Iraq is already in a state of turmoil," he told Kellerman. "The air campaign has reversed its industrial history by fifty years, its civil services nearly as much. We leave things as they are and internal warfare is going to displace thousands of people, and the damned

Kurds are going to get their asses kicked like they always do, which means refugees along the Turkish as well as Iranian frontiers with nothing to sustain them. Are we prepared to deal with that?"

Sam Kellerman yawned. He'd been around the Washington scene for years. A staunch Republican he'd become entranced by the infighting and skulduggery of the capital's political machine. He didn't see people anymore, just opportunities. Countries outside his own were intangible pawns. Some were more powerful than others. All were meant to be exploited for the greater good of whoever was in power in the White House. America was what counted. The rest of the world could either get on board or be run over. "We *want* turmoil in Iraq, Conrad," he explained. "Iran is becoming moderate once again. They need us and we need them. Saudi Arabia is firmly committed to a U.S. presence, joining Egypt who we indebted to us by canceling their deficit of umpteen million dollars. King Hussein fucked up by tying his turban to Saddam's wagon, but then again he's so corrupt it wasn't much of a surprise. We'll square Jordan away once the war's over, just wait and see.

"Syria is positioning herself as a major player and we need her help in getting the hostages out of Lebanon. Tit for tat, there. Israel got the message: no more money if you don't play by our rules, so they played. The point is this. We're in the best possible position to bring about peace in the Middle East. Everyone there now knows we carry a very large stick. It behooves them to talk to each other if we suggest that might be a nice gesture. Arab unity has always been a joke—just witness Saddam's call for a holy war when this mess started. No, we want that fool in Baghdad to worry about his own backyard while the rest of the region is redefined politically. His influence is kaput, his image one of a consistent loser when it comes to gathering the tribes around his cause."

Billings's belly was grumbling. With a start he realized it was time for lunch and he had already missed breakfast. "Wonderful," he told Kellerman. "George gets his best shot at solving the age-old crisis of the Middle East. That coup ought to ensure a Republican in the Oval Office for a few years to come, especially if we add the release of the hostages in Lebanon and hang one of Hussein's best hatchet men to boot. Am I getting the big picture, Sam?"

Kellerman slowly nodded. "Right as rain, Connie. Now, can your boys get Ali Hussein or do we need to rely on our other assets?"

"Thornton can do the job, providing your intelligence people don't fuck up. We're already running around Iraq like it was Disneyland; what did 'The Bear' call it . . . 'a special operations theme park?' "

"Right. That's Schwarzkopf for you, always got a great one-liner for the droolers in the media. We're pinning Colonel Hussein down now, hoping to take him either in Baghdad itself or once he's moved his new command further north. Word has it he's going to be responsible for shutting the Kurdish problem down."

Conrad waved a hand, wishing he'd eaten earlier. "Best man for the job. That'll put him in Kirkuk for starters. They've got a fucking airport there so he can use whatever air power is left."

"I'm impressed at your knowledge of the area," admired Kellerman. "Saddam's still got his gunships and a few fixed-wing aircraft hidden out in bunkers. Our boys blew up some of the easier ones to get to on the ground, particulary those around religious and historic sites. If I were Ali I'd want to be in Kirkuk myself."

"Thornton's team is still aboard the *Curtis*. I want them to stand down operations until this thing comes together. They've been working round the clock since the air war kicked off. I need David Lee linked back up with Bo. He's presently running a TOC in Turkey for the Tenth. Any problem?"

"None. Do what you need to. We're already working with the Kuwaiti ambassador on how to go about turning Colonel Hussein over to him once the team makes the snatch. I've asked the SOC CinC to ready a cell for him in

Kuwait City. None of our Arab 'allies' are willing to hold one of Saddam's kinfolk in irons, for obvious reasons."

This time it was Billings's turn to laugh. "No shit? I understand Iraq's got a special forces unit of their own, trained by the Russians and fully capable of coming and going as they please. Sure as shooting—pardon the pun— if old Sheik Whats-His-Nuts puts a relative of Saddam's in the pokey we're gonna see heads rolling in all the royal families!"

"That's why Kuwait is our only logical choice," replied Kellerman drily. "We let the Emir and his people do the honors, then get on with business. Let Thornton know to expect a launch date within a few days. Time is of the essence, Conrad. This thing's going to be over with sooner than anyone expected. We've got to strike while the iron's hot and the people are still behind the flag. You need anything, call me personally. Anyone gumming up the works will find his ass digging latrines in one of those refugee camps you're so concerned about."

"Always a pleasure doing business with you, Sam," said Billings as both men rose and shook hands.

"Enjoy your lunch, Connie. I'll let the President know he can count on you as always."

"Thanks a fucking lot," responded the suddenly disgusted point man for Springblade.

"Don't mention it," laughed Kellerman. "To anyone . . ."

# CHAPTER
# 6

Colonel Ali ibn el Hussein pulled his red beret snugly onto his head, tugging and forming the symbol of Iraq's special forces so that it conformed to his skull like a second skin. His uniform was clean and smartly pressed, a highly polished belt of black leather buckled around his waist. A pair of metal parachutist wings were tightly pinned above his right breast, a bright row of ribbons above his left. His boots were polished to a mirror finish, and on his left hand he wore a heavy gold ring given to him by his cousin, the president of Iraq. Reviewing himself in the full-length mirror provided as a courtesy by the president's staff, Hussein assured himself he wasn't the worse for wear, despite the harrowing journey from Kuwait to Baghdad.

What he'd seen along the corpse-laden route had shocked him to his very core. Iraqi soldiers were fleeing like frightened rabbits from the front, Republican Guard troops unable to turn them around and in some cases fleeing northward faster than their cowardly brothers. American air power had turned the highways into corridors of twisted and burning death, long convoys from Kuwait devoured by A-10 "Warthogs" and F-15 fighter jets. Refugees were a common sight as well. Shell-shocked and hungry, the masses were fleeing the inferno of Basra where Shiite Moslems were turning captured weapons on Iraqi troops. Everywhere there was destruction and confusion, and the continuing air raids were making travel nearly impossible.

But he'd made it despite the obstacles, Allah be praised. The state of the capital was revolting, to say the least. The colonel had never seen precision bombing like the Americans, British, and French were conducting it. Civilian casualties were low, though the propaganda machine was attempting to inflate the figures in the vain hope of shaming the West. Military targets were burned-out shells, power and water plants ruined beyond repair. There were no bridges standing across the rivers, merely pontoon crossings thrown up by Iraqi Army engineers, and they were available only to military traffic. Baghdad was on its knees, and its leader had been forced to live underground; there was no question the forces of the coalition wanted him dead by any means.

Returning to the city, Colonel Hussein had lost half his bodyguard. The remaining men were quartered nearby, although above ground. Of Captain Ibrahim's fate the colonel had no inkling, but privately he hoped the officer had also escaped the ferocity of the battle for the city. If he was so fortunate Hussein would hear from him shortly. One could always use a dedicated killing machine like the captain.

Crossing the carpeted floor the colonel pulled a thin cigar from an open box on his newly acquired desk. Lighting it he drew in a deep, double lungful of pungent smoke and savored the pleasure of the moment. Saddam was prepared to meet with him at any time. His cousin was rapidly regaining control of his forces now that Schwarzkopf had announced a cessation of offensive operations. One hundred hours! In such a fleeting measure of time the entire Iraqi effort to secure and occupy Kuwait had been torn asunder. To the colonel it was an act of superior military planning and logistics. The American commander had mounted a daring sweep around the Iraqi flank, driving his armored forces deep into Iraq, cutting off the troops in Kuwait, and ripping through the highly regarded Republican Guard as if they were beginners. But to stop now? Why, in Allah's most wondrous name?

Sitting behind the desk, Hussein pondered the thought process he imagined might be taking place in the Bear's lair. The man could crush Iraq within the week, that was a given. Once the Kurds rolled down from their beloved mountains the northern portion of the country would fold due to the the lack of a coherent command chain and the nonexistence of supplies and air power. Basra in the south was already lost; the Shiites were being supplied from captured stores and aided from across the Iranian border. In addition, the Americans were solidly entrenched in southwestern Iraq. Anyone caught in the middle was a casualty just waiting to happen.

So why stop now? It made no sense. If it had been Hussein in charge they would have rolled happily along until the gates of the capital had come down. It was a bad decision on the part of someone in the coalition, or was it?

Puffing on the cigar, the colonel realized that Iraq had become a political puppet. It was all suddenly very clear, and very cynical. Blasted from the outside the country would be thrown into an internal disorder so cataclysmic that Iraq would take years to even begin to recover. They had been conquered as surely as if coalition tanks had indeed occupied Baghdad's streets, but now they were to be humiliated in the eyes of the world as not even being worth the effort to hold.

It left a bad taste in the officer's mouth.

The soft knock at the door drew his attention away from the realization that Iraq was once again a tribal battlefield rather than a regional power. "Yes, enter!"

The door opened slowly and the imposing figure of President Saddam Hussein entered the room. Like a shot the colonel was on his feet, heels clicking together, back ramrod straight, hand held in a tight salute. He had not expected his cousin to make a personal visit and was therefore startled and not just a bit afraid. "Sit," commanded Saddam. "Your journey was long and hazardous so I thought it polite to meet with you here rather than in my office."

"His Excellency does me a great honor," proffered the colonel. "I pray you are well and blessed by God."

Hussein nodded slowly, raising a hand in acceptance of the cordiality extended by his cousin. His face was drawn, the eyes sunk into the massive skull as if the man had slept little in some time. He was always smartly attired and today was no exception. A simple battle uniform snugly fitted his slightly pot-bellied frame. There was a Browning Hi-Power riding on his hip. A second weapon must be hidden somewhere, as Saddam always carried a backup. The colonel wondered how the man could maintain his composure, given the circumstances.

"How can I be of service to His Excellency?" asked the suddenly nervous officer.

"You did well in Kuwait, cousin. I read your reports and inspected what you sent back from the Emir's shoddy regime. The television tells of the fires you ordered set, of the spill in the Gulf as well. They say Kuwait City is a wasteland, a place which will take years to rebuild. That pleases me.

"The forces against us have stopped their attack. Why?"

Hussein shook his head. It was dangerous to be too frank with his country's ruler. Untold hundreds had died over the years for speaking the truth on any given issue. How ironic it would be to die in Baghdad at his cousin's hand after surviving the horrors of war. "Perhaps they see there is more to gain by leaving Iraq crippled, Excellency?"

Saddam glared at the officer, turning his blood to ice. Then the snakelike stare softened and was replaced with a strangely introspective look. "Indeed, we are fighting each other, of that there is no doubt. The wretched Kurds are taking advantage of my weakness in the north, the Shiites have risen up against me in the south. It would be easy if we had an air force left, but Iran—may they burn in Hell—has refused to return our planes. So you think Mr. Bush wants me to stay in power a while longer, eh cousin?"

The colonel only nodded his head once.

"Damn Bush and his Arab lackeys!" Hussein leapt to his feet, a throbbing plainly visible at the base of his throat as the blood in his veins was pushed at warp speed to his enraged brain. "They lied when their woman ambassador told me the United States wouldn't interfere in our dispute over Kuwait's illegal occupation of our land. They lied again when Bush said he would send troops only to defend the Saudi whores who became women when we occupied the nineteenth province, like Saladin of old. Now Bush decides to keep his word and occupy only Kuwait, leaving Iraq crippled and ruined, at the mercy of her neighbors and the laughing stock of the world!"

Hussein was in awe. The president was shaking with rage. His temper was legendary among those who'd survived the many purges he'd conducted, sometimes on a whim. It was certain his cousin might order him shot simply to ease his pain at losing yet one more test of moral superiority. Better shot than beaten to death, as others Ali knew had been. "Excellency, at least you still command the country. Have we not won the war by surviving the onslaught of the world's greatest power?"

It was twisted logic, but what the fuck, thought the desperate Special Forces officer. What could his cousin do, send him to Kuwait?

Suddenly Saddam was in command. As if the colonel had doused him with a bucket of ice water the fire was gone, replaced with a brutal air of understanding. "Yes! Of course we have won! Bush is a coward because he refuses to bring the battle to a close. He fears me! I have defeated the world by staying alive, by ruling Iraq despite everything they have thrown against us. Let them sit in the desert and puff out their chests! We have a great deal of work ahead of us, Colonel. Come! Let us plan our future over lunch."

*Allah be praised,* sighed Hussein to himself. If he could only wrangle a command somewhere far from the capital there would be less chance of falling out of favor. "Excellency, a moment of your time before we eat?"

President Hussein nodded, sitting calmly in a huge leather chair and crossing his legs. He was fully concentrated on his cousin, completely in command of himself and those around him. It was Saddam's great strength that he could draw upon hidden wells of patience and cunning. That was how he'd come to rule Iraq in the first place.

Ali began, choosing his words carefully, laying out his thoughts one by one. "Excellency, the Americans are content to fulfill their promise to force us only from Kuwait, not from power in Iraq. It would seem our first task is to exert military control over our own people again. Your intelligence people have advised me that we have lost little in terms of our armor and infantry in the north, along the border with Turkey. Likewise, the southeastern portions of the country retain great stores of fuel and ammunition."

"What you say is true, so far," offered Saddam. "Go on, I hear your words, cousin."

The colonel pressed onward. "Loyal army units and the Republican Guard can muster the strength to retake the south. I advise shuttling what air reserves are left northward, with Kirkuk our primary objective. If the Kurds are successful in cutting off half the country they may install a provisional government. Such a government need only claim administrative control of the area before being recognized by the United Nations."

" . . . If this happens the rebels could ask for military assistance against us, is this what you are suggesting?"

"Quite so, Excellency. The UN would have to consider such a request, and the coalition would be forced to enforce a favorable ruling. It is obvious they do not want to triumph over us now; so would their policy change if the Kurds are successful?"

"No, of course not," agreed Saddam.

"I propose we accept whatever is being offered by Schwarzkopf, stalling for time, of course. We need the helicopters to fight the rebels, so a ruse must be given to keep them flying without interference.

"Should we disengage from all external hostilities, the coalition will have no choice but to leave us to our own devices. American mothers and fathers want their children home safely. Why fight Iraq if Iraq refuses to fight?

"Finally, give me a command in the north. I will take only the Special Forces and Paratroop units with me. The Kurds need a lesson in humility which I am prepared to teach them. Kuwait taught me many new lessons in dealing out the justice of His Excellency. With what is available I promise to push the rebels out of the cities they have taken and back into the mountains. Many will die; many more will flee. Let the Turks and Iranians deal with the refugees as they will threaten the borders by the thousands. We need the country as a whole, Excellency. Allow me the opportunity to prove my worth and loyalty to you once again."

Hussein sat immobile, his eyes locked onto those of the colonel. A thick, violent silence enveloped the room the two men occupied. Ali held his breath, forcing himself to appear calm and collected. His cousin could smell fear, sense it like a wild animal. When he did, suspicion arose, then paranoia.

And paranoia with Saddam Hussein was a death sentence.

"Your loyalty has not been a question with me," assured the ruler of Iraq. "No one was more capable than yourself when it came to subjecting the Kuwaitis to my will, no one stayed in harm's way longer when the final curtain began to fall.

"Your words have merit, and your plan is good. I will issue the necessary orders giving you control over the units you request. It will take some time to notify their commanders; we are forced to rely on primitive communication means due to the effectiveness of the bombing.

"Take Kirkuk first. The airport is vital to our plan if we can pull the wool over the Bear's eyes concerning our air assets. Arbil must be next, with Rayal a good place to push the rebels and their families. With Iran just across the frontier many of them will flee to the east, forcing our enemy to deal with them. The same with Zakhu. Use Mosul to the south as a jumping-off point once you have retaken it. The Turks have blessed this disaster upon us; let them absorb our garbage as you push the Kurds northward.

"Finally, tell me of what you left in Kuwait for our enemies there to deal with."

Colonel Hussein was stunned at the swiftness with which he'd been granted his wish. He'd be gone from Baghdad by tomorrow afternoon, taking his chances with the rebels rather than with his government's moody leader. "Kuwait? Oh, the Palestinians? We left huge caches of arms for them, scattered throughout the city. So many helped us destroy the infrastructure of the Emir's government that retribution against them is certain. My men trained many Palestinians in urban warfare, setting up guerrilla cells and providing communications equipment so they might maintain a united command. Unless the coalition moves quickly these marauders will begin a civil war much like that seen in Lebanon."

"Excellent!" clapped Saddam. "Do you predict such a thing happening?"

"The process is in place. Everyone sees the Palestinians as an oppressed people. They do not imagine how much they helped us, especially after Your Excellency invited them to fight alongside us. No Arab country but Jordan made them feel important. The Kuwaitis will seek to avenge themselves on those they sheltered for so long and who, in turn, betrayed them in their darkest hour. The media will report such violations, and we shall be free to solve our own internal problems as the eyes of the world once again turn upon Kuwait's lack of 'democracy.' "

"Are you still hungry, Colonel?"

"Famished, Your Excellency."

Saddam Hussein, the Butcher of Baghdad, arose and extended his hand to his faithful cousin. "We eat well in the bunker," he said. "It is one of our few pleasures."

# CHAPTER
## 7

Warrant Officer Francis "Frank" Harrington slowly rubbed his swollen eyes, feeling the grit which was like sandpaper between the orbs and the eyelids supposed to protect them. Harrington was a Special Forces warrant officer, assigned to the newly reactivated Third Special Forces Group stationed at Fort Bragg. At battalion strength the unit had been deployed to Saudi Arabia, assigned to the Special Operations Command base there.

The drive into Kuwait had been swift. Predrawn battle plans were now being changed like a baby's diapers. Special Forces personnel were being deployed throughout the theater of operations, charged with scooping up POWs, intelligence, rescuing Kuwaiti hostages, and securing tactically important sites. Harrington's team drew an ambush, and had been dropped via PAVE-HAWK into southern Iraq near the town of Al-Amarah. Reports of Iraqi special units seeking to escape the anger of the coalition's forces and using the town as a safe haven were circulating back to the CinC at Central Command. The detachment's mission was to scout the area and snatch anyone who looked promising. If that was impossible they were to simply terminate the targets and file a report. End of mission.

His people had been onsite for two days, infiltrating during the early morning hours when it was still dark. Carrying H&K SVD 9-mm submachine guns, the team was also armed with a variety of grenades, knives, and automatic pistols. Those toting the issue Beretta 92's were further blessed by having issued suppressors, matching the units on their SVDs. A few elected to carry the tried-and-true Colt .45 Government, which had been in the inventory for over sixty years. They had one sniper system with them, a modified M-16 with suppressor and ART scope. All told, they were capable of engaging a force twice their size.

"You seen them red berets yet?" A tired Southern drawl drew the officer's attention away from the shimmering sand which was beginning to drive him somewhat mad. The speaker, Staff Sergeant Jerry Johnson, was his relief. They'd agreed to maintain two-hour watches during the day. The intensity of the sun and the boredom did not allow for any more than that. Buried in shallow holes, using chickenwire camouflage covers hastily fabricated after they'd inserted, the team worked in two-man teams, a tiny perimeter formed in the wasteland of Iraq.

"Not since they snuck in last night, Sarge. Iraqi special forces by the uniform, probably beatin' feet outta the city before we could rope 'em off." Harrington wiped his nose on a well-used drive-on rag, stuffing the filthy scrap of green cloth back down his sweat-starched fatigue shirt when finished.

Johnson, pushing his patrol cap back on his head, silently agreed. "They can't hole up in town for too long, ain't safe. Figure them to move out by nightfall, heading for the capital."

"Sure as shit Basra isn't safe," commented Harrington. "All sorts of fighting going on there."

"Hold on!" whispered the sergeant. "Maybe our boys are getting a bit uptight."

Peering through his shrouded binoculars, the officer could clearly see Captain Ibrahim's tattered band preparing to move out. The men were a hard-looking lot, not at all like those the SF team had been plinking for fun since the beginning of the ground war. "AK-74s, plenty of grenades, an RPG-7 with rockets, handguns, bayonets, knives. I'd say these boys are loaded for bear, my man."

"I'll alert the others," said Johnson. "Jamie can thump a few from here with his '16; we can waste the rest once they're clear of the ville." Like a large sand-colored crab, the NCO backed out of the field-expedient hide. His excitement was infectious, and Harrington felt the adrenalin begin to surge.

Ibrahim checked the worn map in his hand for the final time. They'd been fighting for their very lives since leaving Kuwait City, each hour a struggle for survival as every chance encounter turned into a firefight. First it was with the Iraqi Army itself, stragglers hungry for food and desperate enough to attack their own brothers for it. Then came the Resistance, sharpshooting them from the tops of buildings and from behind sand dunes near the beach. There'd even been a shootout with British commandos—where they'd come from Ibrahim didn't even want to know. Most of their journey had been on foot, since vehicles were sure death. The American pilots cruised the skies just looking for something moving to kill.

It had not been a fun trip for the SPETSNAZ-trained officer.

"Pack it up and let's be gone," he ordered harshly. Three days of beard covered his face. His eyes were watery and stinging from the heat of the day. Normally he'd have elected to move at nightfall, when it was both cooler and safer. But everyone was jumpy, eager to be heading deeper into their homeland toward safety. Besides, the town was a target, and soon enough their enemies would come rolling in with their huge tanks and personnel carriers. In Allah's Blessed Name he hadn't seen firepower like what they'd faced since dropping the colonel's command center with several hundred pounds of plastic. The Iranians were nothing compared to the armored columns of the Americans, who shot first and asked no questions afterwards.

"The men are ready, Captain." Corporal Ahiz attempted a half-hearted salute, deciding it was unnecessary halfway through the motion.

"Take point, Ahiz. I'll be in the middle of the file with the radio. Watch carefully, and move quickly. I want to cover five kilometers between now and nightfall before we rest."

The scout nodded his understanding, cocking the AK-74 quickly and locking the safety into position. "It must have been a nice place to live before the war," he said to no one in particular.

Ibrahim glanced around at the stucco buildings, noting the fearful eyes peering at them from deep within the guts of the structures. "Perhaps," he said. "For now it has been an oasis for Saddam's loyal troops. Let's move, Corporal."

"They're gonna walk right into us!" hissed Johnson. "Damn point is moving out like he's on fire." The Special Forces operator eased the blunt snout of the SVD forward, drawing a bead on Ahiz as the Iraqi began to set a blistering pace away from the already forgotten town.

Harrington couldn't believe their luck. Iraqi Special Forces in the motherfucking open! He hoped his people would hold their fire until he initiated the ambush with a magazine from his own SVD. "This is one for the history books," he whispered to his weapons sergeant. "Now let's just let them get a bit closer so we bag the whole gaggle."

Johnson smiled. His patrol cap was turned around backward so as not to interfere with his vision. "I want one of them berets," he intoned. "Look mighty fine hanging up in my war room back home." Tracking on Ahiz he mentally figured how many rounds to put the man down with before moving on to another live one. *Just like shooting turkeys back home*, he thought. *Nice big dumb Iraqi turkeys.*

Ibrahim heard the familiar chugging of the silenced SVDs even as Corporal Ahiz began to fall. Shouting for his men to take cover, the Iraqi officer knew they were finished. The ambush had sprung less than fifty meters off their left flank. Rolling in the hot sand, he cursed his stupidity. Who would have thought there'd be danger this close to the town? Rising up, he fired half a magazine toward the camouflaged fighting positions. His unit was up against professionals, to judge by the way they were cutting the Iraqis apart.

"Grenades!" yelled one of the Green Berets on Harrington's right flank. Ducking his head as he changed magazines the warrant officer heard the dull *thump!* of an object landing to his rear. The explosion threw sand and rock through the air at high velocity.

"All overthrown!" screamed Johnson. "Watch the RTO, he's trying to make a break for the ville!"

Ibrahim vainly tried to jerk his radio man back down beside him, but the soldier was too crazed with fear to heed his leader's warning. Bolting to his feet, he began running toward the town, dumping the radio after three hurried steps so as to lighten his load and extend his chances of making it. The first round caught him in the side of the head, spilling a load of frantically computing brain matter into the absorbent sand. A burst of fire spun the lifeless corpse around so Ibrahim could see the shocked look of wonderment in the man's face, a final pounding of 9-mm slugs ripping the sunken chest apart as the body collapsed in a heap of dirty clothing and shattered hopes.

"God is great!" yelled one of the remaining Iraqis. Ibrahim watched him die as well. It looked as if the colonel would have to fight the Kurds by himself, cursed the doomed officer. Slipping a fresh magazine into the well of his assault rifle, he chambered a fresh round and prepared to die.

"Gonna pop the dude in the middle, boss." Sighting in on Ibrahim, the operator squeezed his weapon's trigger and felt the rounds head downrange as the gun emptied its magazine.

"You got him!" shouted Harrington. "Shot the hell out of his weapon too." Rolling over, the officer began yelling for the team to cease fire. The ambush had been successful; every Iraqi engaged was clearly in view and down for the count. Blood pools were everywhere. No sound came from the bodies as the coalition commandos gingerly left the safety of their hides and began checking the results of their kill-fest.

"Watch that fucking town!" ordered Johnson. "And no one picks up nothing until we're sure all these rat-bastard motherfuckers are dead!" In teams of two the Green Berets rapidly searched the dead men's pockets and packs, snatching up documents and code books, ignoring the gory mess their rounds had made of the once-elite Iraqi soldiers.

"Got a live one over here!"

"Rank?" asked Harrington, running to where the man lay. Two SVDs were pointed at the Iraqi's bleeding head.

"He's a fucking captain, Frank. Was in front of their RTO when we blasted them. Looks like his weapon took the brunt of the battle; maybe the stock bucked him in the head. Anyhow, he's down and out for the count. Wanna kill him or take him home?"

Harrington knelt down on one knee, carefully rolling the wounded man over. Jerking the Iraqi captain's identity book from a buttoned breast pocket, he quickly scanned its contents. "Shit-fire," he spit. "This is one of the dudes our S-2 wants in a bad way! Captain T. Ibrahim, Iraqi Special Forces. I'll be go-to-hell!"

"Who the fuck is he?" questioned the sniper named Jamie.

"Freakin' headhunter from Kuwait City, you dumb asshole. The ragheads want his ass for war crimes; he's a frigging 'Dead or Alive' kinda guy with the Kuwaitis. Ain't that right, Frank?"

"Bandage him up, tie him, gag him, and get me a HAWK ASAP," ordered the warrant officer. "We're outta here with one to go. Make sure security's in place. Tell whoever you get we need a gunship or two."

"Gonna smoke the ville?" asked Johnson, his trophy beret stuffed safely inside an already-too-full cargo pocket.

"One shot our way and that's an affirmative," replied Harrington. "I'm betting though they just close up shop and wait us out. No one wants to die anymore, not even for old Saddam."

"Choppers inbound, Frank! They say we got about a twenty-minute wait but they're burning up the sky to get to us. I told them about Ibra-what's-his-name. That seemed to light a fire back at the shack."

"Nice touch, Ronnie. You boys want goodies, take 'em now. I want the weapons that aren't damaged; everything else stays. We move out in two minutes. The bird can exfil us a coupla hundred meters away from this bitch."

"We got a good one here, don't we Frank?"

Turning to his grinning weapons man Harrington nodded. "He's medal material, Jerry. You got a beret for me?"

Laughing, the seasoned desert raider jerked Ibrahim's blood-stained beret from beneath his now-secured body. "Compliments of the team, sir. Wear it in good health!"

# CHAPTER

## 8

"His name is Tarik Ibrahim, Captain, Special Forces. Team from the Third wasted his unit inside southern Iraq. Seems the good captain here is wanted for a number of things by our allies, the Kuwaitis." Frank Hartung handed the tiny military ID book to Thornton, who confirmed Ibrahim's grainy black-and-white photograph with the bandaged man sitting in front of him.

"SOC CinC were on their toes," commented Bo. "Guess Billings got the word out to all the right places concerning our mission."

Hartung grunted his agreement. "Mr. Harrington and his people are being squared away below decks. We can hold on to them for the duration if you think we need some backup. Been a long time since I've seen the Third's flash in action."

Thornton nodded. Harrington's unit had been recently reactivated under the Special Ops Expansion Program. At only battalion strength, they'd deployed to the Middle East—the first combat deployment in the group's history, to Bo's knowledge. He knew the commander, a Special Forces veteran with hard time in Central America in the early 1980's. A lot of blue chips stacked up in the career officer's favor, according to sources at Bragg. "SEALs are running back-to-back missions as it is. Vejo's people are dog-tired and we could use some fresh muscle, at least during the insertion. Fill Harrington in. Ask if he would like to give us a hand. We got a Arab speaker available to chat with the good captain here?"

Sipping at his coffee, Frank shook his head. "Be another few minutes. I like the idea of having a team go in as cover, especially if we need to get pulled out under fire. Washington likes to come up with all these balls-to-the-walls plans but they don't have to carry the damn things out. Just the intelligence portion is going to be a nightmare. Anyone got a handle on where this colonel is, anyway?"

"Negative. Best guess is Baghdad with his cousin the president. Radio intercept has preparations being made to send a sizable force into northern Iraq to begin operations against the Kurds. Some town called Kirkuk is mentioned, although it's currently under rebel control. No names, but units being scrambled are airborne and special ops in nature."

"That fits our target's character. Kirkuk is the perfect jumping-off point for further ops into the mountains and around the Turkish border. There's an airport that'll service heliborne forces, and it's a good place to gather up armor assets. Maybe old Ibrahim here can help us out, once he comes to."

Standing, both men took a hard moment to examine their catch. Flown directly out of Iraq to the *Curtis*, their prisoner had been drugged, and his wounds had been tended to by Harrington's medic as well as the ship's doctor. Ibrahim's file wasn't complete, but it was noteworthy. Kuwaiti Resistance forces had gathered what information they could during the occupation concerning notable personalities like the Special Forces officer. For the time being, Thornton's team had the man, to use in the furtherance of their mission requirements. They had orders to return the prisoner to SOC CinC in Saudi Arabia when they were finished with him. There he would be processed and turned over to the Kuwaiti government for trial. Leaving the cramped infirmary, Bo left orders with the Marine guard that no one was to talk with the POW unless either he or Frank was present. "Let's get some air topside," he told Hartung. "Being around vermin like Tarik upsets my stomach."

It was a gray day aboard the *Curtis*, medium seas running fast and hard, the ship pounding through them as the battle group continued to monitor the Iraqi coastline in accordance with the newly announced ceasefire. Hartung, a cigar clenched between his lips, stood tall against the wind as the ship came about. "No mines today," he observed.

"Fine with me," answered Bo. "Heard someone out there sucked one up yesterday. Any damage?"

"A bit, nothing impressive. Saddam dumped a bunch of them all over the Gulf but we've been snagging them fairly steadily. Nasty warfare, mines."

Thornton sighed, pulling his windbreaker around him tighter as the day's chill bit deeply. "Gotta plan yet?"

Frank laughed, blowing a long plume of smoke out to sea. "I wanna hear what our POW has to say about Hussein. Seems he was one of the last to chat with him before the puke bugged out of the city. If there's a connection between the two it'd be nice to make it. That way we'd have fewer surprises.

"As far as getting on the ground, it's gonna be tough. We can't just waltz that deeply into Iraq without the odds being slightly in our favor of locating this dude. The fighting going on between the government and the Kurds ain't gonna make it any easier, especially if Saddam moves a good bit of what he has left into the AO."

"How about linking up with the rebels in Kirkuk?" asked Bo.

"Now that's an idea worth considering," answered Frank. "*If* we can confirm Ali taking command of the war against the Kurds it would figure he'd head up-country. One thing we know is that he isn't a slacker when it comes to mixing it up. Besides, hanging out with his cousin isn't going to be a lot of fun in the coming days. I'd wager heads are rolling and positions changing as Saddam tries to juggle his government in the face of his worst defeat.

"The Air Force can get us into Iraq, that we know. There'd have to be a launch site set up somewhere out in the desert to jerk us on a moment's notice, but that shouldn't be too tough, given we own the frigging country at this point. I'd say we'd have seventy-two hours on the ground, max. After that the odds are going to drop like the temperature in Alaska on a winter's night."

The two men steadied themselves as the ship dipped deeply in the turbulent sea. "Ever worked off a boat like this before, Frank?"

Hartung shrugged. "Only when we were going into Korea from Japan. Nasty bit of weather then, too. Never wanted to be a sailor. Always thought pounding the ground was a more secure way to make a living."

"I like being on the ocean, myself," offered Bo. "War's cleaner out here; you're more isolated from the daily grind. We go in, do our thing, and come back to clean sheets and a hot shower. Not a bad way to do one's time."

"Yeah," said Frank softly, "you got a point there. I'm thinking of hanging it up after this one, Bo. Thought you ought to know."

Thornton let a brief grin cross his face, salt spray dousing them both as a particularly large wave was split in two by the bow. "Linda and I talked this morning over the phone," he said. "We're going on an extended vacation when I get back. I posted a letter to the President last night, telling him I thought it'd be better if he found someone else to run the project. Jason is pulling the plug as well. Bannion's in for the long haul, and so is Lee."

"Dave's en route from Turkey, you know. Cal told me they expect him to come out from the *Midway* after his plane lands."

"He'd be a good one to take this shit on. Alan isn't ready to settle down, and he'd be a good man to ride the high country with after you're out of it."

Hartung examined his cigar, rolling it gently between his thick fingers. "This was a good war for us, Bo. For the first time since Uncle Adolf we had us a clear-cut badass to deal with. No spook operations like Vietnam, no smoke-and-mirror bullshit like Central America. Just a good old-fashioned conventional conflict with the elected assholes staying on the sidelines while the generals did the fighting.

"It was good for the country, too. I don't give a rat's ass what some pampered half-wit has to say about the rights and wrongs of the Middle East! America has carried the world on her shoulders for years now, handing out money and aid as if there wasn't a bottom to the pot. What'd we get for our effort? Jackshit, that's what. Every ten-penny asshole living in his shithole of a country thinks he can spit in our collective face while still keeping his grubby mitt out there for the freebees. This time around we sent a larger-than-life message to these parasites: Push too hard and take it right up the kazoo!"

"Pretty right-wing of you, Frank," laughed Bo. "What's the point?"

"The 'point' is I've been around the world more than once and this is one hellva way for me to justify hanging up my running shoes. We *won* this one, hands down and no tie score. Oh, the media will whine that Iraq wasn't that tough once all the after-action reports are in. That's all they'll have left, given they guessed this one wrong from Day One.

"But *I* know, and the American people know, we did a fine job over here and at least for a while the strident little voices of the world are going to be a bit more respectful. Old Mao told it like it is when he said 'All power comes from the barrel of a gun.' Maybe it isn't the best way, but it's the way it is unless you're living in la-la land, blissfully protected by others and enjoying freedoms that were handed to you simply because your daddy stuck your mommy in the good old U. S. of A."

"You ain't planning to move to Boulder, Colorado, are you?"

"Nawww, why?"

"They wouldn't like you there, Frank. Trust me."

"Hey! Mr. Thornton! Your Iraqi general is awake and Hector's translator is standing by whenever you're ready." The Navy SEAL stood patiently, a long-bladed combat knife in his hand.

"Thanks! We'll be right down!" yelled Bo. Smiling, the man disappeared into the bowels of the ship from whence he'd come. "Okay, we're both retired after this one's over, agreed?"

Frank Hartung took his best friend's hand, shaking it hard. "Airborne and Amen, brother. You got a great little lady back in Oregon and I got a business to run for the both of us in San Diego. Let's pop this last cherry and call it a career. Calvin and the boys can handle the program from then on out. Me, I'm going home to America."

"You got it, Frank. Now let's go yak with our little buddy, Tarik. We need whatever he's got, and whatever he's got, he's going to give up!"

"I speak English, there's no need for your translator."

Thornton nodded, sending the man away and taking a chair next to Ibrahim's bunk. "How's the head, Captain?"

"Painful, but I am alive. My men?"

From the corner of the room Hartung answered. "They're all dead. You're aboard a U.S. Navy warship somewhere in the Persian Gulf. No one knows your location or status except for us, and no one will unless you cooperate."

Ibrahim pushed himself up on his elbows, staring hard at his inquisitor. "I am a prisoner of war; you must treat me according to the Geneva Conventions, which my country signed." Exhausted, the Iraqi fell back on his bunk, his eyes closed. "I have nothing to tell you but my name and rank."

Thornton glanced at Frank, who only shrugged. "Better clue him in, buddy-boy."

Bo nodded. "Captain Ibrahim, please listen closely to what I am going to say. You're on board a ship at sea. We're involved in special operations, which means those around you are mostly Navy SEALs and Army Green Berets, do you understand?"

Ibrahim's eyes opened wide. It was clear he understood.

"Good," said Bo, "I figured you'd start getting the message. The government of Kuwait wants your ass for war crimes. Shit like shooting civilians, rape, looting, mass murder, junk like that. You're a big name with the Emir and his bunch, big enough that sending you back would make us heroes back home in America.

"Now there's a way you can avoid all the pain and misery that'll go along with a war crimes trial . . . if you ever get to trial, that is. We're looking for an old friend of yours, one Colonel Ali Hussein. You're bad, there's no doubt about that. But the colonel is *really* bad. We want him, the Emir wants him. If you agree to help we might be able to 'lose' you along the way. Play the Iraqi war hero routine and it's off to Kuwait City in chains."

Fear in his eyes Ibrahim struggled to maintain his weakening composure. "You cannot do this! I demand to be treated according to the Geneva Convention! You cannot threaten me in this fashion, I know my rights under international law!"

Hartung came unglued, pushing past Thornton and screwing his face within an inch of the now totally cowed Iraqi. "Listen up, fuck-nuts! That freak in Baghdad you call a leader has put our pilots on television, their faces battered beyond recognition and their lives clearly at stake if they don't say what they're told to. Don't hand me any crap about your 'rights,' because Bucko, you ain't got any!

"Now here's the drill. We're gonna ask you questions and you're gonna answer them to the best of your limited ability. You lie, you die. I don't have to wait for some Arab courtroom to know you're a punk butcher stuffed into a fancy uniform. A soldier you're not, mister. Soldiers live by a code that's stricter than any civilian law I know of. What you are is trash, garbage, shit.

"So let's cut the bullshit, Captain. We're going to find your freaking boss and drag his ass back to Kuwait. They're gonna hang him, pure and simple. You want to save your butt, start talking. You want to find out what it's like playing the little woman to half the Kuwaiti Army, keep playing the fool . . . that is if I don't slit your throat myself and feed you to the fish!"

Tarik Ibrahim was silent. The American's words were not strange to him; in fact, he understood the message quite well. They were talking his language after all, the language of death unless an end was achieved. Tarik had spoken this way to many, many prisoners. And he had kept his word. To cooperate was to live for a few more moments in the sun. To refuse was to die, often badly, always alone.

He made his decision. "I want to disappear. New documents, new life. There is no one in Iraq to mourn me, no home to return to. Hussein would see me dead once he learned of my 'cooperation,' so I agree to help you *if* you do the same for me."

Thornton looked at Frank. "If what he's got is good, I don't give a shit what happens to him after we get back. You?"

Hartung looked hard at the Iraqi officer. "We have to clear it with our higher-ups, but unless what you know is a hundred percent accurate, your ass ain't worth a hoot in hell to us."

"I know where the colonel is, if he escaped Kuwait alive. I was to meet him in Baghdad with my men. He was planning to meet with President Hussein, his cousin."

"Why?" pressed Thornton.

"The war with the West is over, that we knew. But a new war goes on inside Iraq. Colonel Hussein plans to destroy the Kurdish rebels, he needs the victory to remain in his cousin's good graces. I was to help him. My talents are useful in such matters. We made a plan before he fled the city. I know its details. If you help me I shall return the favor, as Allah is my witness."

"Call SOC CinC," ordered Bo. "We need a command decision ASAP."

Ibrahim fell back on his bunk. For him, the war was over.

# CHAPTER

## 9

The tank poked its long tube around the street's badly damaged corner. Unseen eyes inside the thick steel turret searched for something to kill. A bit of fleeting movement from down the block caught the gunner's attention, and his response was a long stream of green tracer fire which only added to the destruction of Kirkuk. Satisfied there were no hidden rocket men waiting for it, the tank crawled forward. A puff of dirty smoke erupted from its exhaust stacks, a bit more pollution for the guerrillas to breath as they fought Saddam's vengeful army.

As a battle it was fairly one-sided. Colonel Hussein's armored columns had driven the Kurds out of the residential districts and outlying communities, forcing them into the city, where fierce house-to-house fighting became the order of the day. The paratroopers had to be trucked in because of Schwarzkopf's unconditional demand that no fixed-wing aircraft could fly, but they were blessed with air cover anyhow. Hind gunships were happily butchering the rebels whenever they could be caught in the open, which was all too often. Acid was dropped from makeshift vats built into the cargo areas, bombs were dumped by hand, and thousands of antipersonnel mines were laid down. Heeding what they believed was a call to arms by President George Bush, the Kurds had mounted hugely successful attacks all over northern Iraq. The problem was they could not maintain their revolution against the unholy president called Saddam, not without massive assistance from the outside.

Which was never to come.

The colonel's plan was simple. First, he would drive the Kurds out of Kirkuk and the other major populated areas of which they had gained control. With administrative control regained the army could concentrate on securing the all-important oil facilities which were needed to fuel their war machine as well as for economic support. Saddam, sick of the Kurds' constant uprisings, had given the go-ahead for his cousin to push as many of the bastards out of Iraq as possible. With Bush apparently choosing to ignore the valiant mountain tribesmen it was open season; the Iraqi Special Forces conducted daring raids into the mountain strongholds or called in helicopter air strikes and artillery whenever large groups of Kurds could be pinpointed.

They were killing thousands of men, women, and children with no interference from the outside. After all, it was an internal matter as far as the coalition was concerned.

The colonel was coordinating the battle from a mobile command post just outside the city. So far they'd managed to dislodge the primary Kurdish combat units. Prisoners were not taken; those were Hussein's orders. When Kirkuk was under control once again they would begin blasting away at the mountain villages, driving the people from their homes and, it was hoped, across the borders of Turkey and Iran.

Hussein was studying a map when an aide tapped politely at the door to his trailer. "Colonel, the tank commander offers that his unit has breeched the rebel defenses at the northernmost portion of the city. Should he proceed further, or attempt to link up with those driving up from the center?"

Colonel Hussein smiled broadly. Their progress was encouraging, although the cost was somewhat high. Rebels with captured RPGs had destroyed a number of tanks and personnel carriers at the outset of the battle. He'd requested Republican Guard units to deploy immediately, a request which was granted as soon as it was received. As the untouched Guard forces vented their rage at being so deftly defeated by the allies, the assaults gathered momentum. Their orders were to the point—kill Kurds wherever they might be found. "Have him deploy his tanks where they stand," he ordered. "They will seal off the last avenue of escape for those still in the city. Concentrate all units on their objectives. I want Kirkuk in our hands by nightfall!"

The aide saluted, turned, and ran for the communications van to relay the most recent orders. Finally, he thought, we are winning a battle!

Hussein returned to the map. He had armored columns moving up along the Iran-Iraq border, their objective to quell any thoughts of rebellion which might be simmering along that front. Most of the Kurds were encamped between Turkey and the northwestern portion of Iran. With a pincer movement along the Syrian border complementing the drive this side of Iran, it would be possible to merge the tribes and clans in one central area. At that point they could simply lock the doors and begin slaughtering the rebels at will. Turkey couldn't handle millions of refugees storming across the rocky frontier, and Iran would surely send her army to push the filthy scum back once the weight of the tide became too much.

Personally, Hussein was ecstatic that the allies were leaving the Kurds to their own devices. He understood their caution about extending support; the difficulties of attempting to work with the Afghan resistance must have been a grim reminder that such efforts often went unrewarded. The Kurds, interested only in obtaining a Kurdish state of their own, historically accepted aid from anyone who offered it. The Soviets funneled thousands of pounds of military supplies to them, and the Iranians picked up the slack whenever the Russian well went dry. One could not hinge any long-term political hopes on the Kurds, who felt nothing for anything other than the establishment of their miserable little foothold of a country. They were as much a tool of the Arab world as the Palestinians when it came to hiring out an entire nation to raise hell with one's neighbors.

A volley of automatic weapons fire told the officer another batch of rebels were on their way to Allah. Tribal warfare was nothing new to Iraq. As a matter of fact, it was a respected tradition. Upon taking power Saddam Hussein had succeeded in melding the country into a powerful whole. He'd kicked out the British, who'd dominated the area for years, and he'd forced Turkey to abandon her plans to gobble up the country. Kuwait, reasoned Saddam, was part of greater Iraq but for the whim of the British, who had drawn an irregular line in the sand between Saudi Arabia and Hussein's homeland. What was critical was the desire of the British not to leave Iraq with an open waterway to the Persian Gulf. Their being thrown out of the country was masterminded by Brigadier Abd al-Karim al Qasim, a man who Saddam would attempt to kill in his early quest for power. As punishment for their losing face, the English effectively landlocked the Iraqis, leaving Iran, newly formed Kuwait, and Saudi Arabia with access to the all-important sea-lanes. It was a bitter pill for Iraq's leadership to swallow.

The map showed their vulnerability as clearly as a clear sky reveals the sun. Colonel Hussein poked a dirty finger at Jordan, the Iraqi's only lifeline to the Mediterranean Sea. King Hussein (no relation) had stood steadfastly by Saddam, urged in part by the fact the monarch's kingdom was bellied up against Israel and populated by a huge number of displaced Palestinians. Iraq was always a possible ally against an invasion by Israel, a trump card the king might need.

Both Syria and Iran possessed military forces capable of defeating Iraq. Indeed, the eight-year war with Iran had bled Saddam's legions and coffers dry. Saudi Arabia had thrown its lot in with the Americans, although Hussein always believed they could have taken the country within weeks after occupying Kuwait. The Saudi army was a posturing bunch of overdressed fools, commanded by ineffectual officers and totally inept at actual warfare. Iraqi intelligence had reported that the Saudis were ripe for the taking, but Saddam had waffled at the thought, preferring to consolidate his forces and claim Iraq wanted only what was historically theirs.

To the colonel's way of thinking it had been a serious blunder.

The roar of a gunship distracted the officer. Thank God for the Hinds, he thought. Matched up on the ground, the Kurds were proving effective in small-unit combat operations. Without air support the fighting would have been much harder, even with armor available to the Iraqis. Hussein enjoyed flying the occasional mission with a gunship, especially when it caught the rebels with their pants down. You could kill a lot of people in one pass, and many more when there was nowhere to run and hide. He'd ordered the crews to take advantage of the masses of humanity gorging the narrow roads leading to the borders. The only good Kurd was a dead Kurd, he'd told them. Damn helicopters took a lot of bullets to support, though.

"Colonel, we've raised flag downtown! Kirkuk is once again ours!" The aide's triumphant smile was catching, as Hussein's staff cheered their commander, slapping each other on the back and promising to show the rebels a thing or two wherever they raised their heads.

"Refuel the tanks, restock the Hinds. I want everyone ready to move forward by first light. Order the units coming up behind us to fill in the lines. I want the paras airlifted by Hind & Hip forward by ten kilometers. The battle is over, but the war is not!"

The men responded quickly, their joy in serving a relative of the president coupled with their fear of being shot, skinned, or sent to a combat unit "up front." Kirkuk was taken, praised be Allah.

# CHAPTER
# 10

"If I didn't know any better I'd swear you were a buncha goat-eaters from deepest, darkest Iraq." Hartung laughed loudly at his own joke, enjoying the scene before him. Briskly rubbing dark-brown skin dye onto every exposed portion of their bodies, the men were preparing for what the trade referred to as a "black operation."

Black-ops aren't new to the world of covert warfare. Historically they've been used successfully in any number of conflicts, from all-out wars to not-so-simple tribal conflicts. American special operations began paying attention to the technique after the Rhodesians proved the black-op was an effective means of accomplishing those missions normally considered politically suicidal. The Selous Scouts roved across Rhodesia's borders wearing the enemy's uniforms, their skin dyed as black as that of the guerrillas they were fighting. A ruse, the key to such a tactic lay in the enemy being unable to prove who it was who ruined their day. Black-ops also allowed one to get in close, initiating contact on often surprised elements of the "bad guys" before they could react with any force or accuracy.

"Frank, I *still* think we could find a place for you on the MH-47 if you *really* wanted to go." Mike Bannion, his shoulder-length blond hair dyed coal-black, began rubbing a handful of the skin dye onto his massive left forearm.

"Your momma's big ass, son. I'll be in the air all right,

flying nose-gun in one of them new 'Super Cobra' gunships the Army's so proud of. Besides, I look terrible in anything other than my own natural color."

Thornton finished applying a generous coating of the oily stain to Jason Silver's face. Stepping back, he admired his handiwork, touching up spots where the former ranger's pale skin was peeking through the bark-colored pigment. "Ya look just like an Iraqi warlord, my boy. Suit you up in one of them captured uniforms and you could stand next to old Saddam himself and go unnoticed."

Silver managed a bleak grin. "Lee get in yet?" he asked.

"Bird's inbound as we speak," answered Rowe. "How do I appear?"

Harrington, watching the team suit up from a semi-comfortable spot in the corner of the room, shook his head. "An oriental Iraqi is simply bizarre. All you guys are bizarre. Who the hell do you work for and can I get a job application?" The room filled with laughter, a pair of dirty socks striking the warrant officer square in the nose.

Grabbing a newly "liberated" AKM assault rifle, Frank checked its action, feeling the oiled bolt carrier group slide back and forth without a hitch. "We do the Lord's work, Mr. Harrington. We come from a land far away to deliver the Lord's message of love and forgiveness to our enemies."

"And if the enemy isn't listening . . . ?"

"Then we kills his deaf ass," finished Bo. "The Lord is patient but he cares not for the stupid. Frank, throw me a uniform that fits from that pile Hector brought in!"

As Bo slipped out of his jeans and began trying on the camouflage uniform of an Iraqi paratrooper, he watched the team go about its business. They'd drained Ibrahim of everything he had, putting him under the needle just to confirm that what he was telling them was true. There'd been a few lies, but not many and of no account. Hartung had stayed behind after the interrogation ended officially, wanting to fill in some blanks.

"How's our special farces asshole doing?" asked Thornton.

"He proved to be as big a sore on the face of the earth as I thought," remarked Frank. "I asked about some of the shit he did to the Kuwaitis, as well as others I might add. A real scary piece of work, that one. Colonel Hussein sure knew how to pick his henchmen. I thought I'd heard it all until Ibrahim came around."

Bo buttoned up the baggy trousers, slipping into a loose fatigue shirt and admiring the nearly perfect fit. It was nice having a sewing shop on board. The SEALs were physically much larger than the Iraqis and needed alterations when it came to dressing like the enemy. "Too bad we had to cut a deal with Tarik. Guy like that should be facing his victims instead of picking out a new passport and heading for freedom."

"I wouldn't sweat that happening," commented Frank.

The room grew still, all eyes on the two men. "Where's Ibrahim?" asked Thornton. "Where is he, Frank?"

Hartung stood, stretching. After a moment he put his arms down, rubbing the smooth grips of the Colt .45 he'd carried on and off for over thirty-some years of both hot and cold combat. "He went swimming after you'd left."

Bo stared hard at his friend. "Murder, Frank? You killed the poor son of a bitch just because he was a freaking human slaughterhouse?"

Nodding, Hartung lit a cigar. "Seen too many of them boys walk away from their responsibility to society, son. Korea, Southeast Asia, Central America, you name the war and I'll show you someone who got his rocks off hurting people for the fun of it.

"Old Tarik was one of the best. Took babies and played 'stick the bayonet' with 'em, then raped their mommas and killed them too. Herded old men into elevator shafts filled with explosives and blew them apart. Played with little girls until he was bored, then gave them to his men. Bastard robbed and killed and raped and burned everything he could get his hands on. Kuwait was a playground for him.

"So, yeah, I tossed him overboard when no one was looking. Give a whore's son like that a second chance at life? Let him ride off in the sunset a free man while my best friends are heading inland, maybe for the last time? Spend the rest of my life like Chuikov did, *knowing* I had the chance to stamp out a piece of human filth like Ibrahim and didn't do it?

"Nawwww, ain't gonna live that way. Tarik had a date with the devil and I made sure he made it on time. End of mission."

Bo was on his feet, the veins in his neck standing out, his anger at Frank's action clearly visible, almost tangible. "I gave the man my word. He gave us what we needed to pull this mission and I promised him a way out. It was *approved*, Frank! It was a done deal!"

Hartung hadn't moved. The smoke from his cigar was curling up in a lazy spiral, its odor filling the room as surely as Bo's unbridled emotions were. Not a muscle moved, not an eye blinked as the men watched and waited for the cards to be laid out. "Bo Thornton, you did indeed give your word and God knows that word is good.

"But, I didn't give mine and you didn't ask for it. You didn't kill the silly bastard, Frank Hartung did. Your word to him was good, it was me he should have been having sign on the dotted line."

"That don't cut it, Frank, don't cut it at all," replied Thornton. "It was *my* decision, *my* word. You had no right cutting in like this."

Frank nodded slowly, his eyes hooded. "It ain't a question of giving your word, Bo. Never was and never will be. It's *who* you give your word to that matters! There isn't a man on this team who I've sworn to and failed. If there is, he can step forward and say so now."

No one moved. No one dared. No one had to.

Hartung continued. "I've made my point. I give my word to the right man and he can walk into the furnaces of hell knowing I'll be right there at his side. I give my word to someone like Ibrahim, and he might as well go jerk himself off in the corner. You don't like the way I do business, tell me."

Thornton gazed at his friend, hearing what he wasn't

saying far louder than what he was. He could lose the old bastard right here, right now. It was bad enough he'd braced him in front of the team, but he'd included those outside the group as well. Frank didn't care much about saving face, he'd just pack his kit bag and catch the first thing smokin' for the States.

Bo didn't want that. He needed the sergeant-major's wisdom and support, always had, always would. Tarik Ibrahim was everything Frank described. Was he worth losing part of the team over? "Sergeant-Major, I got only one question."

Hartung took a deep breath. "And that is . . . ?"

"Could the bastard swim?"

Frank stared a long moment at the younger man, then a huge smile crossed his features as he realized they'd crossed yet another bridge in their relationship as warriors. "Fuck me to tears, no. Sank like a rock, an Iraqi rock, that is!"

The room exploded with laughter as the tension was flushed away by the two men shaking hands. "Hey, gimmie that dye-shit and let's get this job over with!" All eyes turned to the door where Master Sergeant David Lee was standing, a heavy ruck balanced on one shoulder.

"Yeah!" exclaimed Silver, jumping down from the table he had been sitting on while adjusting the team's emergency radios. "My man Davy Lee is here and ready to get his E-8 ass waxed for no good reason other than he loves us!"

Climbing down the narrow rungs of the ladder, Lee shook hands all around. "How ya doing, Jason? Heard you were selling art up around Bo's shack."

"*Good* art," corrected Silver. "Art with a touch of class."

"The only class you got Silver is the one you graduated from when they let you out of reform school." At Hartung's remark the men once again began exchanging insults, all of them loud and exceptionally demeaning.

Finally Thornton brought the clowning around to a halt. The One-Zero knew they'd needed to blow off steam; the missions being run were almost unbearable when it came to keeping the lid on tight. But now they needed to continue to march, because the hairiest mission of the war was headed their way like a freight train on fire. "At ease, at-fucking-ease! Frank, get Dave squared away and brought up to speed. He's compass man for this gig, Jason on point, Rowe as RTO, Bannion the tail-gunner, and Calvin with me in the middle.

"Mr. Harrington? You need to make sure your team is locked and loaded in case we need an extract in a hurry. You'll be coming in behind us in a second PAVE-LOW, then splitting off with the birds for the launch site until we radio for assistance. Any questions?"

The warrant stood, grabbing his M-16 and tossing off a quick salute. "None for now, Top. I'll get my guys moving and brief you in thirty minutes as to our status."

"Good, we'll be near ready ourselves. See you then."

After Harrington had left Bo turned once again to the men who remained. "Ibrahim gave us enough to put Hussein in Kirkuk, the first step of his plan to bash the hell out of the Kurds. Intelligence has a confirmation on Hussein meeting with his cousin, Saddam, a coupla days ago. Everyone knows what's going down in northern Iraq. We're dumping a load on the rebels and that ain't no shit. They're hanging on but there's no reason to believe they can pull it off without serious-business support from our side.

"Men, it ain't coming.

"We're going in tonight, flying one hundred feet off the deck with no lights and no sirens. There'll be four gunships with us, plus Harrington's MH-47. A KC-130 is gonna meet our task force somewhere over the desert and pass some gas to keep us flying. Someone has engine trouble, they go down and get picked back up by elements from SOAR 160. We lose two birds en route and the mission is scrubbed.

"Plan of attack is to infil near Kirkuk, playing ourselves off as Iraqi commandos. We find the colonel by grabbing anyone unlucky enough to be nearby and asking hard questions, fast. Dave speaks the lingo, that's one of the reasons he's on board. There *is* no HUMIT available past the frigging coastline. Agency sources are scattered all over hell, and those in Baghdad are being used as little as possible."

"But we know this Hussein creep is definitely at the front, right?"

"Roger that, Jay. Radio intercept has him pegged in the city as of yesterday. He's gonna consolidate his forces before pushing toward Arbil, which is the next logical rung on the ladder."

"What if we can't make contact?"

"We get an early out," said Bo. "Seventy-two hours on the ground without the colonel and we be history.

"Now the question comes up about what we're gonna do if we can't yank this bad boy. I asked Conrad over the SatCom for a sanction and Bush refused. This is a declared war and just like we couldn't go after the head honcho himself, we can't expect to get the word to terminate his cousin either.

"But, this is combat, and strange and wonderful things happen on the battlefield. *If* Colonel Hussein makes himself a viable target, and *if* one of us has the opportunity to make him die for his country, then certainly the proper response is in order. The Administration can live with that. *We* can live with that. Questions?"

"Someone gets hit and can't get out?" It was Alan Rowe, an Iraqi paratroop smock hiding the power of his tightly muscled upper body.

"We all go in, we all come out. No one gets left behind. Shit happens, we all know that. If it's me on the ground I want one of you bastards to put a round through my skull before you pull pitch. I'll do the same for you."

Silver's hand popped up. "Any chance of linking up with the rebels if we need the firepower?"

"The Kurds are as prone to shoot us as they are the Iraqis. Maybe more so, given our lack of support when they needed it most. We've all worked around the locals enough to know you can't second-guess them. The option is open; we'll ride that pony when the time comes."

Frank grunted. "You need to understand we're gonna be camping out in the boonies waitin' on your asses. Hard to say if Saddam's boys won't accidentally run into us, or spot us from the air via his choppers. Air Force is gonna fly mucho missions to try and confuse things in the general AO. Lots of overflights, shit like that. Remember, we *ain't* supposed to be in Iraq doing the bad thing. There's a cease-fucking-fire on . . . although you wouldn't know it if you're on the rebel side. We got to go, that's the gig. E&E is a very real thing on this one, boys. Don't go losin' your compasses."

"I love it when you talk like that, Sergeant-Major. Where's the nearest Red Cross, Bo?"

Thornton jammed a magazine into the well of his Browning. "Cal, I think we'd best figure on heading up the mountain toward Turkey, just like the rest of the Kurds. Dave's been working a launch site over the border so there's good guys in the area. That means a chance of being extracted, or at least found. Our radios are good for the distance, and I've got codes for making commo with the Tenth if we have to."

The room was quiet except for the sound of men preparing for war. Thornton left them alone with their thoughts, watching as each took a moment to help the other, a touch of reassurance here, a gruff comment and laugh there. They were the best, the stone-cold, no-holds-barred best. Beaumont "Bo" Thornton said a silent prayer of thanks to the good Lord for letting him be a part of their special fraternity. Then he started loading magazines. It was killing time again, and Colonel Ali Hussein was the man of the hour.

Allah be praised.

# CHAPTER

## 11

The Kurd named Haziz stepped back and surveyed his handiwork. The disabled truck *almost* blocked the steep single-lane road which wound its way like a writhing serpent up into the mountains of northern Iraq. Hidden in the ground were a half-dozen antipersonnel mines, each cleverly camouflaged so it was invisible to the human eye. The vehicle itself was wired with explosives as well, a steel coffin for whoever would attempt to use it as cover once the ambush was sprung.

Satisfied, the rebel leader barked a curt command to his men. The group nodded, huge smiles on their faces as they contemplated how many Iraqi soldiers they might have the opportunity to kill before the day was out. Of course, the number would never equal the pain and injury Saddam could inflict with a single gunship attack, but it was the thought that counted.

Haziz watched with approval as the men, most armed with Soviet weaponry, clambered up the steep hillside and into their shallow positions. Carving out a place from which to fight was difficult in the mountains, especially with so little available in natural camouflage. As the Kurds hunkered down to wait, their leader put a pair of captured Iraqi binoculars to his eyes and swept the area below.

Ten miles to the south lay a devastated village. Hussein's Republican Guard had first used helicopters against it, strafing and rocketing the town for three straight hours. Afterward, they'd poured in artillery fire. High explosives to begin with, then mustard gas. Many who'd lived through the first attack became victims of the second. Finally, after the winds had blown the gas clear, Iraqi infantry and armor made their appearance. What hadn't been destroyed was looted. Those who hadn't been killed, were. The children watched their fathers and brothers butchered in the shattered streets, their mothers and sisters brutally raped by laughing soldiers who felt no pity and offered no mercy. Those who were left packed what they could salvage and began the trek toward the border, life as they had known it smothered by Saddam's legions.

Sweeping westward, Haziz nodded at the softness and beauty of the fertile fields, now untended. Such a lovely country, he thought to himself. When the sun was high and the work hard there was no better place to call home. The Kurd was originally a farmer, a man of the soil. His natural inclination was to till the earth, to prepare it for the growing season, and to pamper it and prune it as the crops began to sprout and mature. Finally there would be the harvest, the payoff for all the hard work. So long ago, he was reminded.

Today he was a guerrilla commander. His family but for one son were all dead. His farm lay in ruins, his life gutted by the madman in Baghdad. He vividly remembered the very moment he'd put down the implements of peace to replace them with the tools of war. It was the saddest day of his life, but also the most rewarding. He would fight to be rid of Hussein, and he would lead his friends in the struggle. A respected man, Haziz quickly assumed responsibility for the underground war in his district. The Iraqis grew to know his name and to fear it. The Kurd's mouth twisted into a vengeful smile as his glasses picked up the slow-moving convoy of vehicles, the flag of Hussein clearly visible on the lead armored car.

Shortly he would fertilize the hard roadway with the blood of the Iraqi invader, his act one of love and determination; the honor of his people was the crop to be reaped.

Haziz the farmer turned to his restful men and waved.

Death lifted her skirts and leered lewdly at the unsuspecting Iraqis, their vehicles beginning the long climb upward.

The air was still. Only the heavy drone of industrial-size engines could be heard as the ambushers adjusted the aim of their weapons for the hundredth time. Small droplets of sweat peppered each man's face, the heat of the day bringing it up through their pores like a prophet raising the dead. Flies, drawn by the sour odor of the men's body grease, feasted without fear as their hosts forced themselves to ignore the buzzing, thick-bodied pests. The Iraqi column was cautious, poking and sniffing its way up the mountain at a snail's pace. They knew the Kurds roamed northern Iraq at will. The litter of those less fortunate was commonplace along the roadways. Burned trucks and bits of tattered uniform material were grim reminders of the war within Saddam's own borders.

Haziz fingered a thick-bladed bayonet at his hip. He'd personally taken it from a Russian advisor killed in an ambush not unlike the one in place now. The man had fought bravely, whereas the Iraqis had fought our of sheer terror. Captured, Haziz elected to execute the man quickly, as a warrior. The others of the Russian's command were toyed with for hours, their pain and humiliation a delight to the battle-hardened Kurdish guerrillas. He'd kept the knife as a trophy, sharpening and honing the tough steel until it cut silk cleanly.

"Brother, I see their lead soldiers . . . there!" Pointing with his finger, the Kurd directed his leader's gaze onto a lone Iraqi soldier who had just looked up and seen the battered decoy vehicle broadside in the roadway. Although he was more than one hundred meters away, Haziz noted the look of surprise in the man's face, knowing he would scamper back to inform the column's commander of this potential danger point.

"We wait," was all the guerrilla chief said. "Make no

movement or sound. The Iraqis will send out a patrol to check the road for mines. They will investigate the truck, curious as to why it is there in such a position. When the first soldier detonates a mine, the men down the mountain will seal off the road using their machine guns and rockets. Then we will have our just vengeance on these animals!"

Five minutes elapsed before the Iraqi patrol appeared. The men were wary, their heads swinging to and fro as straining eyes attempted to detect the slightest hint of danger. Hands gripped tightly around their assault rifles, they inched forward, leg muscles stiff with anticipation, heartbeats rapid. Overhead, large, black birds soared on the thermal air-currents coming off the mountain's side. Insects were chirping. Somewhere a wild dog barked playfully at something he was chasing. Still the Iraqis came forward, their truck engines at a steady idle where they sat hidden by the abrupt bend in the road.

Haziz gently pushed his safety downward, muffling the distinctive "click" the AK made with his hand. His breathing was shallow now, loaded with anticipation and scented with the urge to kill. The hillside was devoid of any trace of the Kurds. Each man had reverted to his innermost nature as a hunter. As one they waited out the Iraqi advance, knowing any movement or sound would betray them.

Below, the first soldier stopped and knelt on one knee. He was wearing the standard deep green of the Iraqi Army, a faded black beret cocked on his head. The man's assault rifle moved slowly across his front, its barrel an antennae seeking out the signals which would bring on a burst of automatic fire. The soldiers behind the scout had spread themselves out on the road, each searching the hillside for any sign of ambush. The sun's glare hampered their efforts; the broken-down truck was a massive distraction to the men. Where had it come from? Who had died in it? How would they move it to continue their journey? These and other questions were crowding their minds, sapping their combat instincts of the necessary edge they needed to detect the Kurdish trap.

"He has seen us!" hissed the Kurd burrowed in next to Haziz.

"Silence, idiot!" whispered the guerrilla. "He sees nothing but rock and dirt! Hold your tongue before I hand it to you myself!" The Kurdish rebel smiled a moment at the instant obedience of his follower. They were good men, he reminded himself. Men whose homes were vacant or destroyed, men whose families lay cold in the ground or were shivering from the lack of blankets in camps along the borders. Soldiers they were not, freedom fighters they were. He was proud of each and every one, a pride he showed when telling tales of their bravery around the campfires at night.

"They move . . ." advised his comrade-in-arms, his voice under control again.

The Iraqi scout stood, his right hand raising as he brought the tiny patrol forward to inspect the damaged vehicle blocking their progress. As the men stepped into the mined ring of the obstacle, Haziz held his breath. Sooner or later one of the dolts would have to trigger a mine, bringing the wrath of the Kurds down upon them in a hail of not-so-divine jacketed intervention. A team of sappers was positioned where they could observe the temporarily halted column. Buried in the earth were several pounds of explosive, enough to cause a small rock-slide behind the column, forcing it forward and into the waiting jaws of the Kurds' ambush. When the first antipersonnel mine exploded, the team would drop thousands of pounds of rock on the roadway, then begin firing into the rear of the Iraqi column. There were ten vehicles in all, and perhaps fifty soldiers. It would be a great victory, with much loot, if they could pull it off within the next few seconds.

*WHHHUMMMPFFF!* The mine erupted in a fireball of shrapnel and bits of earth and rock. The unfortunate Iraqi who'd triggered it was tossed over the precipice, most of his left leg gone as well as both forearms. His scream was short-lived. His head cracked open on a jagged bit of granite when he bounced the first time. Haziz thought the whole thing quite entertaining as his AK began to spit death into the shocked band trapped in his sights.

A massive explosion rent the air on the attacking Kurds' left flank. Alerted by the mine, the sapper team eagerly detonated their own charge, which sealed the Iraqis' rear exit off in a dusty waterfall of split rock and shale. One of the guerrillas let loose with an RPG-7. The rocket slammed into the last vehicle of the column with an ear-splitting shriek. There were no survivors as the truck began to burn. The popping sound of exploding ammunition echoed down the steep canyon.

"God is Great!" roared Haziz. The steady *thrump-thrump-thrump* of a Kurdish-manned RPD light machine gun washed over the rebel chieftain like cool water. The soldiers were hidden by a veil of exploding mines and expended cordite, the booby-trapped roadblock becoming a death trap for them as they attempted to seek cover from the rounds sent downrange by the rebels.

"The trucks are moving our way!" screamed a Kurd further up the hillside than his commander.

Haziz quickly dumped his empty magazine, ramming a full one up the AK's belly and chambering a round with a furious snap of his hand. Drawing a bead on the windshield of the lead armored car, the Kurd began working a string of rounds up across its glaring surface. A crew-served gun atop the vehicle began roaring back in anger, its first few rounds killing two rebels as they attempted to bring an antitank round on line with the car's exposed flank. Haziz began praying that his men could at least disable the speeding Iraqi war machine, since it possessed the brute power necessary to push the decoy truck out of position, thus effectively breaking the ambush apart at the seams.

Suddenly the sound of a rocket in flight reached the Kurd's hopeful ears. The RPG slammed dead-center into the vehicle, blowing it open in a rush of ruptured fuel lines and shredded metal. The armored car spun sideways, then rolled up on its side as the second truck in line swung hard to the right to avoid a collision. The Iraqis were trying to fire from the open beds of their rolling coffins. Most of the rounds hit nothing but the mountain's dry dirt. There were eight trucks left, and their drivers realized as one that there was no way out of the nightmare around them.

"Grenades!" ordered Haziz, leading the way by tossing two in a row into the road. The air was then filled with the arm-launched bombs. Some fell gracefully into the backs of those trucks closest. Others skipped and rolled harmlessly off into the ruined landscape below. Individual explosions announced the grenades' effects, as sprays of blood appeared like hot-steam geysers. A knot of Iraqi soldiers were successful in dismounting their vehicle, the driver of which was a headless corpse thanks to a burst of rifle fire from one of his own panicky men. The group huddled up against the truck and began laying down a base of fire against the Kurdish freedom fighters. Its intensity was enough to slacken the rebels' outgoing steel so that more Iraqi soldiers could find cover.

"Kill them!" screamed Haziz. "Kill them before they can rally!" His own AK was red-hot, a growing pile of empty magazines growing under his aching arms as he poured round after round into the killing zone.

Without warning the Kurds around him broke cover and began running downhill. Haziz envisioned their total destruction, but found himself also on his feet, yelling at the top of his voice and racing against the wind toward the Iraqi position. A tug at his hip told him he'd been hit; another bullet burned a bloody furrow across his belly. Still the Kurd raced forward, dropping the empty assault rifle and pulling the razor-sharp bayonet from its scabbard.

The Iraqis couldn't believe their eyes. As the first rebel collided with their fragile perimeter they balked, allowing a moment's lapse in their fire so that the man was able to breech the ring before going down in a storm of high-velocity lead. In seconds it was hand-to-hand combat all along the ragged line. Filled with tribal hatred, both sides fought without compassion, killing each other in a frenzy of bare steel and hot lead. Guttural oaths filled the air, the sick sounds of chopping coupled with the hard *whack* of wooden rifle butts striking yielding flesh. As gasoline tanks exploded around them the mass of enraged humanity fought on, each side determined to destroy the other or perish trying.

Then it was over. Wounded, bleeding, but still able to walk, Haziz began to rally his men. The survivors were finishing off the wounded, Iraqi voices pleading in vain as single shots rang out above the roar of fuel fires. Black smoke from the burning truck tires was choking the rebels, blinding them as they searched the battlefield for their own wounded comrades. Haziz knew he'd lost more men than he could afford. His victory was hollow because of their zeal to close with Saddam's butchers. "Hurry," he ordered. "Kill the living and recover what we can. Soon the helicopters will arrive. They can see this smoke for miles!"

Within ten minutes the tiny band was ready to disappear into the hills. They'd left ten of their own, warriors killed in a holy war against a regime dedicated to their extinction. Over fifty Iraqis lay dead, their bodies a grisly message for those who would be tasked to clean up the ravaged scene.

"Where to?" asked one Kurd, a blood-soaked bandage wrapped around one hand.

Haziz grimaced at his own wounds which were burning like Hell's own fires. "Up into the mountains," he said simply. "We have no place else to go but the mountains." With that the guerrilla leader took the first of many steps toward safety, his men falling in behind him, rifles once again locked and loaded, eyes alert, souls in anguish for those they were leaving behind.

The war in Iraq continued.

# CHAPTER
## 12

Thornton took a moment to adjust the Browning on his hip, touching the dull black suppressor with a fingertip to ensure it was tightly screwed onto the 9-mm's barrel. The rest of the team was standing several feet away from the forceful commando, checking each other's equipment and making small talk as they waited for the PAVE-LOW crew to extend an invitation to load the bird. Bo gazed out across the enormous flight deck of the *Midway* as the *Curtis* moved slowly away from the aircraft carrier after transferring its cargo of human torpedoes to their launch site.

"Penny for your thoughts," offered Hartung.

Thornton nodded in the darkness. "Heard the ground troops are kicking the living shit outta the goat-eaters," he said.

Frank, snugly dressed for the evening's chill, laughed. "Old Saddam just plain fucked this one up, that's all. His boys have been getting slammed on a regular basis since the air war began, but that isn't what's costing him troops."

"What then?" asked Bo, tugging his camouflaged smock tighter around the throat.

"No will to fight for the cause," answered Frank. "Bush gave the dumb bastard seven months to prepare a defense. You don't think he didn't order some serious bunkers built? On top of that, there's more than enough food and water been trucked in or taken from the Kuwaitis. Nope, they just don't believe Kuwait is worth dying for, and that's why they're giving up as soon as they see a chocolate-chip uniform in the distance."

"Heard the pilots are starting to have a bad time," said Bo.

Frank shook his head in the affirmative. Since the ground war's beginning the Air Force and Navy pilots had been killing thousands of Iraqi soldiers as they scurried around Kuwait looking for a way home. "Heard the same. Pilots say it's a turkey shoot, just aim your guns and let loose til the well's dry. The Iraqs ain't even firing back half the time, just sucking up rounds. Our boys have never been cold-hearted killers, so I don't doubt they're raising the issue."

"This one's gonna be a bitch, Frank. You know that, don't you?"

The retired sergeant-major studied the man beside him for a moment before answering. He'd fought with Bo Thornton in Vietnam and knew what the One-Zero was capable of. Later, they'd earned their keep battling against the insurgency in El Salvador and Honduras and assisting the Contras in Nicaragua. The deal with the Oval Office hadn't been an easy affair. Every mission was just a bit more complicated than the one before. Kicking ass in Iraq was at least an aboveboard war, for that Frank Hartung was grateful. "Want some advice from an old 'operator,' Bo?"

"Makes you sound like you work for Ma Bell," quipped Thornton. "So what's the recommendation, you old coot?"

Frank jammed his hands down into the depths of his jacket. "This Hussein thing is all well and good, catch at least one of the really bad guys and see justice done, or what passes for justice. Problem is *we* have to pull it off first.

"Now this colonel is going to have boo-coo security wrapped around his ass, count on it. Plus, there's the rebels as well as possible Iraqi assassins out to get their licks in on one of the royal family should the opportunity present itself. Getting close enough to grab Hussein isn't going to be the breeze our boys back in Command Central figure it.

"My suggestion to you is this. You get close enough to put the cross hairs on our boy, zap him. Bringing Hussein back alive is going to cause a hatful of trouble for everyone, especially the Kurds."

"How so?"

"We grab Saddam's kissin' cousin, he gets pissed and grabs about a thousand men, women, and children from a group of people he hasn't any use for anyhow. Give back the colonel and they go free. Try him for war crimes and watch the grave diggers go to work in the central park of Baghdad.

"It's a given, Bo. Our government doesn't truly understand a man like Saddam. Why be the reason for another buncha refugees dying just so the political clowns can get a few notches on their belts? Grease the silly puke, call for extract, and let's go home to Linda, eh?"

Thornton drew in a deep breath of clean sea air. Linda. He hadn't seen her for months. They talked once a week over the ship's SatCom link to the States, but he missed her touch, her smell, the feel of her after a good night's loving. "Kinda making our own rules again, aren't we Frank?"

"Rules?" coughed the veteran Special Ops sergeant. "There ain't any 'rules' over there," he said with a broad sweep of his hand. "They *slaughtered* more folks than we're ever gonna find during the occupation. *We* slaughtered ten times that many using weapons that fried and dried 'em where they stood. Now they're killing each other in a feeding frenzy of vengeance and retribution. Rules? Whose, pray tell?

"The only edict you can live by is to do the job and come home in one piece with your crew. Ali Hussein is a scumbag. Line him up and shoot him down: there's your justice in one neat package. Lose one man off this team trying to snatch him and you've lost more than I could bear. Do him and be done with it! If the President and his happy band of REMF staffers want a showpiece, let them strap on the guns and get their overweight, overpaid, overrated asses over here and we'll grab a beer and watch *them* die for a change."

Thornton smiled, then gave his friend a quick hug. "Okay, we'll get close enough to pull the colonel's plug and call it a day. War's damn near over with anyhow, ain't worth losing one more American life just to play the hero."

"That's what I wanted to hear," said Frank. "We're civilians, we're supposed to think about shit like this. Remember all those Chinese and Russian advisors we were sent after in Nam? Every time we found one they ordered the poor sucker blown away. Too much embarrassment for our communist friends to have to admit they were mucking around in Vietnam's business as much as we were."

"Point's made, Frank. Just have the choppers ready to fly when I call; it's gonna be a bitch any way you cut it."

Hartung spit on the flight deck. "Airborne and amen, my friend. Airborne and amen."

# CHAPTER

# 13

The MH-47 roared across the desert's darkened floor at less than one hundred feet AGL. On either flank flew a Super Cobra gunship, the dual escort ready to tangle with anything foolish enough to open fire on the speeding aircraft. Already situated at an isolated launch site in northern Iraq were support ships and fuel bladders, all guarded by a platoon of rangers from Fort Lewis. The gunships were being piloted by crews from SOAR 160, the supersecret Special Ops air squadron based out of Fort Campbell, Kentucky.

Inside the bird Thornton's team sat strapped into their red-webbed flight seats. There was no talk between the men, each safely isolated in the maze of his own thoughts. With each bump and rise of the helicopter they took a moment's time to ensure all was well. No one was expecting the big tactical hello to go down, but they did not wish to be caught unaware if there were problems in flight. Every magazine was loaded, every weapon had a round chambered. They'd sharpened their combat knives until each made hair pop off an exposed forearm, the keenness necessary if there was to be killing done up close and personal.

Bo favored his new fighter from Bob Rippy. The gentle curve to the blade was designed to keep the cutting edge in contact with what was being attended to. It was a killing knife, meant to slit a throat or rip a belly, period.

The rest of the team was outfitted with large combat knives. The blades were 5/16-inch thick at the back, with a fully sharpened tip impervious to excessive lateral stress. The five-inch handles were formed from a rubber synthetic called Kraton and was shaped in such a way that the hand didn't slip forward or back during stabs or retrievals. A blackened double guard protected the fingers, and the blade itself likewise darkened using MDS epoxy. At fifteen ounces they were sturdy tools, capable of chopping and slicing their way through anything an Iraqi soldier might be wearing. The edge was flat-ground, making it easy to keep honed to the highest degree possible. Sheathed in black Cordura, each knife was completely sterile, making it acceptable as an issue item for black ops such as the one they were committed to.

Close combat with a knife is greatly misunderstood by the majority of those who study it. Thornton knew the value of having a good edged tool at his side, having soldiered all over the world. Most professionals carried at least three knives in their kits, each specifically assigned one or another task during the course of a mission, or missions.

Tucked into the One-Zero's breast pocket was a Swiss Army *Hunter* model, its lanyard loop tied into a dummy cord which was further tied into the commando leader's pocket flap button hole. The multipurpose folder offered a variety of practical tools, all of which could be used on a mission. If nothing else, the integral can opener was a handy item when laid up sorry (and hungry) in an RON.

Thornton's primary combat knife was the Rippy. Although meant primarily for close-in fighting, the blade's design was open-ended so that it could be used around a campsite if required. The knife was extremely fast in the hand although heavy enough to impart severe wounding when wielded. Bo wore it in a simple leather sheath on his hip, just behind his Browning's holster.

Another edged companion was a double-edged fighter he'd picked up on a trade with one of the SEALs. Made by Ek Commando Knives, the Raider stiletto was a quality reissue of the blade made famous by the Marines' Raider battalions during World War Two. Thornton liked the enhancements and improvements made by the company at the insistence of the Raider Association, which had backed the project with their name. Tightly sheathed in a leather affair replicating that of the original scabbard, the stiletto was purely a tool meant to spill the blood of an enemy. Bo wore this knife opposite his Rippy, preferring the option of taking on a foe with either both knives or just one, depending upon the situation.

Finally, there was the Russian springblade, a ballistic knife which was always worn in a shoulder rig underneath the well-trained soldier's battle jacket.

"Boys are pretty happy with them new bowies sent over," yelled Hartung over the whine of the MH-47's howling turbine.

Thornton smiled at his closest friend and business associate. "Man I respect highly once told me it was better to have two good knives on hand than two guns without bullets. They never jam or run out of horsepower when you might need them most."

Frank gave Bo a thumbs up, returning to his seat after checking each man's combat harness one more time. Buckled in once again, the retired sergeant-major reminded himself that they were flying into hell itself. He was dropping these men—his friends—into Iraq's internal civil war to hunt down a mass murderer, a mission that was damn near suicide. They were good, no doubt about that. And they were lucky, as time had told, mission after mission. But like the old reconner upstairs cautioned, it was better to be lucky than good.

Thornton watched the crew chief as the man spoke a few quick words into his voice-activated mike. His intuition concerning the message sent back from the cockpit was confirmed as the goggled flight specialist made his way down the steel aisle toward the One-Zero. "What's up?" asked Bo.

"We're ten minutes out from the LZ," said the chief.

"So far everything looks good, no camel-jockeys in the immediate AO although there's fighting going on about five klicks to the east."

"Probably the Kurds mixing it up with some of Hussein's bully boys. Are the gunships still gonna prep the area before we go in?"

The man nodded. "They feel it's in your best interests. No one's going to pay much attention to our shit going off, figure it to be just another battle on this side of town. Anything or body who *might* be down there will just get greased, meaning you're in like Flynt without a care in the world."

"Except staying alive," Thornton said wryly. Turning away from the man, Bo tapped Silver on the shoulder. Holding both hands up he gave Jason the crew chief's message, which the former ranger passed down the line in the same manner. They were all wide awake now, the thoughts of thirty seconds ago gone as reality demanded their full attention. Thornton watched Frank begin working toward him from the last man, who happened to be Calvin Bailey. Like the senior jump master he was, the veteran ran his hands and fingers over every piece of equipment being carried. At the same time he was talking a mile a minute, offering advice, cracking a last-minute joke, giving away a bit of comfort to every man on the team. Thornton thanked the Lord he had Frank Hartung on board. It made the mission seem possible.

"Five out!" yelled the crew chief, the fingers of his right hand spread out for Bo to count.

The rear ramp of the chopper began to descend, a blast of cool night air sweeping through the hollow guts of the MH-47 along with the heavy stench of burnt JP-4. As the aircraft's crew began their inspection of the ramp to make sure it was secure, Bo glanced at his watch. They were right on time. The sudden *rrriiippppp!* of multiple miniguns startled all of them as the Cobras began working out on the LZ. Round after speeding round was eating the ground up below, anything living splattered like overripe fruit under the horrific barrage.

"One minute!" roared the crew chief. Hartung was now standing next to him, his monkey-strap secured to a hook in the floor as he leaned out over the rear lip of the ramp to check the ground coming up.

The team was on its feet now, assault rifles slung across their chests, fingers wrapped around wooden or plastic pistol grips, magazines locked, and chambers loaded. The whites of their eyes stood out in contrast to the darkness of their dyed faces and clear desert goggles kept the sand from blinding them as the bird began to settle into its precomputed hover. Thornton knew they were scared, as well they needed to be. But he also understood they were the kind of men who had learned to conquer the negative side of fear. They would use its edge to their advantage, tuning their senses to the highest degree possible once on the ground. Fear could be either friend or foe, depending on how it was channeled.

"Kick it!" ordered Frank. With a deft shove the crew chief booted the coiled bundle of rope clear of the ramp, stepping back inside as Bo grasped the highest possible portion of the now-free line. "Go!" exploded Hartung, delivering a mighty slap to Bo's back as the man swung out into the darkness, his feet wrapping loosely around the thick rope, his hands opening slightly as gravity began sucking him downward.

Silver was next. His heels were inches above Thornton's head as the two men raced for the ground fifty feet below. One after another they hit the line, disappearing into the darkness as the gunships flitted to and fro, looking for anything stupid enough to stumble into the area. "They're free!" yelled Frank. The crew chief spoke rapidly into his mike and the MH-47 responded by pulling upward and away.

"Looks like they're on their way!" said the Special Ops flier.

"You boys do a good job," responded Hartung as both men worked their way toward the unlit flight deck. "Now let's make sure they're moving before we head for our oasis and a bit of hot coffee, shall we?"

Silence. With the MH-47 gone there were no sounds other than a whisper of wind ruffling through the men's clothing as they lay in silence on the sands of Iraq. No one spoke. This was a security check. So far no one outside of themselves had given a hint of human presence. The ground was pockmarked with thousands of thumb-sized craters where the Cobras' guns had tilled the earth. The acrid taint of cordite could be smelled, its taste well known to the team. Thornton, lying next to Silver, who was RTO for the mission, tapped Jason gently on the shoulder.

"Send a SitRep to Frank?" whispered the Vietnam veteran.

"Roger that," replied Bo. "This looks good so far. We'll start moving toward Zakhu in a few more minutes." Jason pulled the handset from where it was riding on the outside of his ruck, keying it, then speaking softly into the black mouthpiece.

Their last bit of intel put Hussein moving on the tiny town of Zakhu, near the border of Turkey. The rebels were reeling from the concentrated attacks of armor and heliborne forces that were swarming over their positions like wolves on a killing spree. Since the air war had been ordered stopped, what little remained of Saddam's own air force was wreaking its revenge on the unsupported Kurdish freedom fighters.

Kirkuk and Arbil were taken within days. Mosul's fate was still being debated, but the outcome in Saddam's favor was decided. Leapfrogging Mosul, Colonel Hussein was racing for the last major concentration of guerrillas who were holed up in Zakhu. If he could recapture the town he would seal the fate of those Kurds stranded between Kirkuk and the Turkish border. Those trying to escape into Syria would most likely perish in the vast wasteland of desert between them and safety, if crossing into Syria could be considered an improvement over Iraq. Refugees and fighters fleeing toward Iran's frontier would likewise have a difficult journey. In addition, they could be pursued and interdicted by untouched military forces scattered throughout northern Iraq.

So it would be at Zakhu that Thornton's team stood the best chance of running into their target. Hussein was on a winning streak. His victories pleased the president, who was stalling for whatever time he could before having to sign the United Nations' conditions for a formal cease-fire. Heads were literally rolling in sunny Baghdad, so those farthest away were the safest, even if high explosive shells were falling all around them, fired by the rebels in their retreat.

"There ain't shit out here," suggested David Lee.

"I'm hearin' you," agreed Bo. "Saddle up, gents. Assume your positions and let's get it on. We need to cover quite a bit of ground before the sun comes up."

The team gained its collective feet, fastening loose rucksack straps and adjusting harnesses and weapons slings as they prepared to move. The plan was to make the outskirts of the town before first light. They'd hole up somewhere, maybe chancing contact with the rebels if it were forced upon them. Bo cursed the fact that no one from the Kurds was available to meet them on the ground. Ground guides were exceptionally helpful in operations like the one they were conducting. They knew the lay of the land, where the enemy was and was not, who could be trusted and who should be avoided. Further, they could act as translators when needed, or make emergency arrangements if things went to hell in a handbasket. If they were to be denied these assets, a total breakdown of the Agency's intelligence network inside Iraq was partly to blame; the other part was the intelligence community's decision to ignore the Kurds as a possible network in the first place.

As a result, what Thornton had was a blind insertion into enemy territory with nothing more than a map, a compass, and someone back at Central Command in Riyadh telling him to "Trust us."

Right.

Bannion moved up next to Bo as the team began humping toward its first map objective. The big man's head was wrapped in the traditional garb of the Kurd, hiding the thick mane of dyed blond hair he wore to his shoulders. "Given any thought as to how we're gonna find this colonel once we get to town?" he asked.

Thornton spit a bit of sand from his mouth. Damned stuff got everywhere, no matter how well you taped and strapped and sewed stuff. "Our 'eye in the sky' is monitoring his radio transmissions, getting a fix from there. We get to Zakhu and Silver will link to the aircraft. They'll fill us in and we just map him out. Piece of cake, Mike."

Bannion giggled, and the sound brought a quick smile to Bo's lips. "I've heard that shit before. It ain't even known if the bastard will be working that close to the border. If nothing else we'll have a chance to see some shit up close."

"Agreed. That's our secondary mission, anyhow. Get some on-the-ground information on what's going on. We got reports of refugees like you wouldn't believe. No one back at the Oval Office really wants to deal with it right now, but we may have to. Kinda tough calling for the good citizens of Iraq to throw the bum out and then leave them in the lurch."

"Poor planning, eh?" offered Mike, his breathing becoming deeper as the sand began pulling at their feet.

"Piss poor planning, if you're asking. All I want is a shot at Hussein, then we're outta here. War's over, battle's won. Who's kiddin' who, anymore?"

Bannion threw a quick look at Bo. "You saying we're just gonna waste the silly asshole instead of . . ."

Thornton stumbled, catching himself before falling to both knees. "Fuck!" he swore under his breath. "What I'm saying," he wheezed as Mike steadied him, "is that Colonel Ali Hussein already earned himself a death sentence. Whether he goes down here, or back in Kuwait City, makes no difference unless you're looking at the public opinion polls before reelection. So yeah, we're gonna shoot the puke on sight. Any problems?"

Mike grinned. "Only one, boss."

"What's that?"

"Who gets the honors?"

Thornton chuckled aloud as the two warriors glided into the night with only the wind at their backs.

# CHAPTER
## 14

Hussein's world erupted around him as the command track was rocked hard by the first rocket impacting against its side. The sound of shearing metal and screaming men deafened him as he was thrown to the hard steel plating which served as the vehicle's floor. Seconds later a line of ragged holes appeared, a heavy machine gun lining its sights up on the wounded track as the rocket team attempted to refit a second missile for the killing shot.

"Out!" ordered an Iraqi noncom whose face was bleeding from a dozen cuts. "Out before they hit us again!" Then he was gone. Only the puddles of blood where the man's wounds had drained gave any evidence he'd existed in the first place.

Hussein forced himself onto his hands and knees. His gut was sickened and he felt the urge to puke this morning's breakfast. The ringing in his ears was increasing. Blood—his blood—ran from his nose and down the sweat-stained paratrooper's smock he'd worn since the campaign had begun. Out. *He had to get out!* Crawling on all fours, the officer managed to find an open exit hatch he succeeded in pulling himself through. No one else was around, in fact, there was little outgoing fire from his troops. Falling hard to the ground, he began dragging himself toward the open door of an abandoned bakery. Behind him the track took a second rocket, this one bursting its sides and igniting fuel from the ruptured fuel tanks.

The day hadn't started off as he'd hoped, recalled Hussein as he rolled inside the ruined shop. In fact, it had sucked, from the moment he'd spilled his coffee when a rebel sniper had nearly blown his heart out while they were preparing breakfast.

*That* memory made him puke.

Gagging a bit, he wiped food-filled drool from his chin and propped himself up against the bullet-marked wall. Zakhu was proving to be a tough nut to crack. The Kurds were defending the town well, sniping soldiers as they dashed from point to point, rocketing vehicles at every corner and with great accuracy. The colonel's men were facing mortars as well. Their indirect fire had been pouring in from the moment the Iraqis had begun their assault. The triumphs of Kirkuk and Mosul were forgotten as Hussein encountered the first stiff resistance of the internal war. His cousin, Saddam, was not going to be pleased.

A flicker of movement caught his eye. Pulling the pistol from its holster, Hussein aimed at where he'd seen the man disappear, not more than ten feet from where he lay. Must have come in through the roof, he thought. Damn rebel had to have been blind not to have seen him there in the open as he was. Suddenly a head, then a body, appeared from behind the upturned counter. The colonel triggered his weapon twice and watched the rounds strike the man hard in the side of his head. Scrambling over to the dead guerrilla, Hussein eagerly pulled a brand new AKM from under him. Ripping the combat harness away as well, he slung it over his shoulders and tightened the straps around his chest so the rig fit snugly. At least I have a worthy weapon now, he reminded himself. Then it was back to the window where he checked the street for his heretofore absent comrades.

There was no one to be seen.

The roof! Hussein, ensured there was a round in the chamber, then made his way slowly up the narrow stone stairway leading to the open rooftop. Once there he peered carefully over its lip, noting with satisfaction that he possessed a clear view of the local battle. A sizable band of his Iraqi paras were preparing to rush what was apparently a rebel stronghold not more than half a block from where he lay. There were no tracks or tanks in view, although he could hear their engines somewhere in the distance. The question was, should he remain in position and simply wait for the block to be taken, or should he attempt to link up with the paras?

With a distant shout the Iraqis were up and running. The officer watched as they gained the middle of the street before the first soldiers began to fall, their bodies spinning as guerrilla bullets knocked them down. But the weight of the attack was too heavy and soon Hussein could hear the sound of heavy fighting going on in the buildings themselves. With a start he realized that the dead rebel downstairs had to have come across the rooftops, which meant more would soon be following as the paras gained control.

Low-crawling across the roof, he found his worst fears realized as the first group of three burst out of an open door two buildings down. They were heavily armed. One carried a loaded RPG over his shoulder. Bringing the heavy assault rifle to his shoulder, Hussein aimed at the rearmost figure. With a loud *pop!* the AKM discharged. The heavy round caught the man high in the chest, causing him to stumble, then fall out of sight.

A wicked burst of gunfire ripped the roofing around him with unbridled ferocity. The Iraqi rolled to his left, then brought the rifle to bear as the two remaining rebels broke cover and began running toward the rooftop which separated Hussein from them. He waited, the weapon now on full automatic. As they began their leap in tandem he fired, noting with glee that he'd caught them both across the middle in one long burst.

As they fell to the street below he changed magazines. A para appeared in the doorway of the house from which the three Kurds had been fighting. With a careful wave Hussein caught his attention . . . and almost a bullet . . . as the man unloaded a full magazine at him. "Idiot!" roared the colonel from behind scanty cover. "Hold your fire or I'll have your balls roasted on an open fire!" Peeking carefully from his hiding place, he was pleased to see several more paras now out in the open, their weapons at ready. Standing up he moved out into the open. "I am your commander!" he yelled, knowing this announcement could earn him a ticket to Allah if fully understood by a Kurdish sniper.

"It is Hussein!" shouted one of the paras whom the colonel now recognized as one of his company commanders. "Lower your weapons! Hurry, Colonel, come across quickly!"

As Hussein made the jump he reminded himself to reward the captain with something after this was over. That is, if he lives through this mess, mused the now-safe Iraqi officer.

"We got a major problem," hissed Alan Rowe. The team had marched all night, reaching the outskirts of Zakhu just as dawn was breaking. They'd scouted an abandoned house and choked down a quick MRE breakfast, washing the mass of precooked food into their famished systems with long, deep draws on their canteens. Lee discovered a deep well inside one of the rooms, and the men replenished their water supplies one by one as Bo stood guard.

"What's the deal?" asked Bo.

Rowe pointed across the narrow street. "Buncha goateaters gathering up on the other side of the road. Couple looking this way with too much interest for my taste. I think they're trying to decide whether to hide out for awhile, or perhaps they need a place to set up an aid station or command center."

Thornton scrambled over to where Alan was peering out the window. Sticking his head up, he saw the Iraqi patrol and counted more than twenty soldiers. "I think you're right," he told Rowe. "Better get ready to receive visitors, gentlemen."

Bannion licked his dry lips and pulled a drum from his ruck for the RPD he was carrying. Moving rapidly across the littered floor, the former SEAL took the high ground, positioning himself where he could cover the street. Rowe and Bailey set up inside what must have been the living area of whoever had owned the now-vacant dwelling. Lee, whose rifle was the only one with a scope, slipped out the back door and crawled to where he could watch their right flank. Thornton and Silver took up positions opposite each other, offering the Iraqis the perfect means to be killed in a crossfire.

Then the wait began.

It didn't last long. "Got movement big-time," warned Mike from his perch upstairs. "At least five scouting the area; the rest are hanging loose, probably waiting to stroll across the street once the house is secured."

Bo grunted his understanding. "They come inside we'll have to take them quietly. Get your blades out! No shots or we'll get pinned down in this shithole. Make it count, gentlemen."

It took the Iraqi recon element another fifteen minutes to sniff the area out. Almost satisfied, they darted one by one from the house across the street, lining up along the wall just outside the team's front door. Inside, the Americans were silent, every knife unsheathed and held low. They'd let the Iraqis enter one by one, taking them as they split into groups to search the shot-up home.

"Incoming!" whispered Bailey as the first soldier rolled into the house. Bailey came to his knees, AKM at the ready.

Silver was already moving, his speed like a striking snake as he tore the man's throat out with a precision slash. A jet of bright red arterial blood squirted from the jagged tear, splashing Jason across his front as he looped his left hand through the dead man's combat harness, dragging the corpse swiftly into the next room before it could fall to the ground.

One down, mused Bo.

The second Iraqi roared into the room like a freight train. Losing his footing in the pool of fresh blood so cordially provided by Silver's bladework, the man slipped and fell, swearing as he went down. A look of horrified wonderment was crossing his face even as Rowe split his skull with the heavy blade. Jerking the blackened blade free, Alan spun as the rest of the Iraqi squad, wanting to escape the unprotected street, pumped themselves into the house.

Thornton stepped into the room, his Rippy held low as he delivered a front-kick to the groin of the nearest enemy soldier. As the man went down Bo grabbed his oily hair, jerking the Iraqi's head upward so his throat was exposed. Ramming the sturdy blade through the soft flesh, Thornton buried the knife to its single guard. With a swift downward motion he tore the blade free, spilling a helmetful of blood over his boots as the man collapsed at his feet.

Calvin Bailey kicked the legs out from under his prey, dropping unceremoniously on top of the man and pushing his knife deep within the Iraqi's heaving chest. The man fought back, digging his hands into Calvin's throat and squeezing it for all he was worth. Bailey concentrated on the knife's quivering handle, leaning forward on the blade with all his weight. He could feel his eyes beginning to pop out of his skull as the enemy soldier raged against death. Together the two men waged a war of wills, each wanting the other dead. Finally it was the Iraqi who relinquished his hold on life.

Bailey rolled off the corpse, puking his guts up as he tried to force air back into his starving lungs. Remembering the knife, he climbed back on top of the body, grasping the Kraton grip with both hands and jerking violently at the big bowie until it was free.

Then he puked again, this time long and hard.

The final scout met his end with the sound of whispering death in his ears. As he leaped into the house Jason Silver appeared, a heavy throwing-knife in his hand. With a flick of his wrist the ranger delivered the knife at high speed and its broad point caught the soldier just below his sternum. Thornton rushed forward, pushing his hand over the dying Iraqi's mouth as he attempted to scream a warning to his comrades across the street. A burst of RPD fire told Bo the jig was up as Mike began dropping long ribbons of fire into the concentrated mass now rushing the house.

"All plans change upon first contact!" yelled Rowe, his assault rifle coming up.

Whipping the Rippy upward, Thornton rammed the bloody blade deep into the dying man's guts. Twisting it, he opened a huge hole and a mass of yellowish-white entrails began to spill out as he pulled the blade free. David Lee's rifle could be heard now. A grenade went off as the Special Forces sniper dumped one squarely into the crowd of oncoming soldiers. "Scatter 'em!" he yelled, stepping clear of the body as it slid to the floor.

Within two minutes it was over.

"Saddle up!" ordered Bo. "Restock your ammo from what these assholes were carrying and let's make tracks!"

Three blocks away one very tired Colonel Hussein perked his ears up at the sound of intense firing coming from somewhere close by. "Now who the hell might that be?" he said aloud. As it died down he declined to dispatch a scout team to check out the source of the firefight. More Kurds we missed first time around, he told himself. Wouldn't they ever learn?

# CHAPTER
# 15

Frank Hartung pulled his folding camp-stool up and accepted the cup of steaming coffee from Tony, the crew chief. Their landing at the launch site had been textbook in execution, the security force lighting the LZ with infrared chemical lights which the MH-47 was able to "see" using its sensor screen.

"Think they'll get him?" The chief sat down on a crate labeled as containing machine parts, spare generators for the Cobras in case they needed repairs in the desert.

"Thanks for the java. How're we lookin'?" Lifting the mug to his lips, he sipped at it gently, careful not to burn the tender flesh as the coffee leaked into his mouth.

His own hands wrapped around a plastic cup, Tony shrugged. "Good, I suppose. No reported sightings of Iraqi troop movement anywhere near us. In fact, everything seems to be headed for Baghdad or beyond. The airframes are tight, no hassles there. We're checking things out, though. Better safe . . ."

" . . . than sorry," finished Hartung. The sun was rising, climbing like a rocket into the blue depth of the sky. By now Bo should be inside Zakhu, or at least at its outskirts. They'd wait seventy-two hours before heading for the primary extraction LZ. If the team wanted to be jerked ahead of time, they'd be on their way within minutes. For now he could only wait.

"This thing's winding down a lot sooner than most expected," said the chief.

Frank turned to the man, whose presence he'd momentarily forgotten. "Huh? Oh, sure. Well, as long as our losses are low and the goal's been accomplished it's okay by me."

Tony nodded. "My dad flew with the First Air Cav in Vietnam. Did 256 missions as a crew chief. Shot down four times, got a Purple Heart off the second one. He flew dustoff, then transferred over to the gunships after getting tired of not being able to shoot back."

Hartung smiled. "Buncha crazy bastards flew with the Cav. They did it all and then some. You can be proud of your old man."

"He didn't want me to join up, but what else was there to do when you come from Nowhere, Ohio? Army's been good to me and the wife; this is my second hitch. Only have ten more years and I'll retire."

Retire. Frank pressed his knees together and shifted his ass on the comfortable old stool. He'd retired. Well, kind of. The shop in San Diego was meant as a capper on his thirty years' worth of government-sent check. The old savings account was looking pretty healthy these days, thanks to the substantial deposits his association with Springblade brought in. But retirement? That hadn't happened yet. "Stick with it, son. You got everything a man needs, plus you sleep clean and fly instead of walk. Not many surefire careers out there in the world these days. Make the most of it."

The younger man stood. "Will do, Top. Want another cup? I'm headed that way. Gotta check the bird out and see what's popping on the net."

"Nope, I'm good to go. Thanks anyway. You brew a good cup of Joe." Frank watched the man amble across the sand toward the chopper they'd flown earlier. He was impressed by the man's confidence and ability. Lot of responsibility riding on his shoulders. Men's lives and a country's future. Too bad more of the whiners back in the States couldn't spend a few hours out here with his kind. Might make 'em think a bit more about their own positions in life.

Hartung reached down and pulled the black combat knife from its sheath. Balancing the knife in his hand, he absently retrieved a sharpening hone from a pocket on his harness and began drawing the already-sharp edge along its fine surface. How many knives has he done this with over the years? It had been an issue bayonet during Korea. Damned thing was dull as a turd when he'd drawn it, and it'd taken hours to pull the edge up to where it would cut cleanly. Once done, though, it wasn't a half-bad killing knife, as at least a few North Koreans and Chinese had found out the hard way.

After that little war he'd bought himself a good hunting knife, but it got lost during a training exercise in Germany. He'd volunteered for Special Forces by then, meeting up with some of the guys in the 10th Group and liking their style. Vietnam followed.

Had some *good* knives there, he reminded himself as he carefully honed the bowie's edge. He remembered being issued one of the old SOG knives while on Okinawa. Designed by Ben Baker of the Counter-Insurgency Support Office (CISO) the knife was hand-forged in Japan by old Mr. Tanaka. SOG had been begging for a sterile knife to run cross-border operations with. The kabar was available but marked and therefore unacceptable. Baker, who'd told the spooks he had more important demands on him than designing knives, relented and began drawing from his personal experiences as well as from tidbits given him by the guys on the ground.

Frank remembered his own knife as having a seven-inch plum-colored blade. SOG operators wanted the longer blade because the knife was meant for close-in fighting, not utility. They needed the length so you could reach in way deep and puncture the vital organs, pure and simple. The Fifth Group caught wind of SOG having its own blade and began yammering for a Special Forces knife. They borrowed Baker's design by adopting the six-inch version that SOG had declined. Instead of a brass pommel and guard, the Fifth went to blued steel with the Special Forces crest stamped into the blade. Both knives used the same sheath pattern, one that put the retention strap opposite the cutting edge so it wouldn't be severed during the knife's withdrawal.

That old SOG knife had served him well, recollected the old commando. He'd carried it all over Vietnam, not to mention a few forays into Laos and the occasional trip to Thailand for some R&R. Quite a few of the men issued such blades simply stored them away in their footlockers as keepsakes. Others traded theirs off, normally to the "Yards," who always needed a good knife. Frank remembered seeing more Randalls and Gerber daggers than the knife made for the Forces, but his had done the job and he couldn't complain.

Of course, he'd "left" it behind in Laos after a particularly gruesome mission. A trip to the PX in Saigon found him toting a big Western bowie, which was hell on wheels in the bush but a bit large for fine work.

Frank lifted the blade to eye-level, examining it under the increasing brightness of the sun. Good lines, a nice grind. Thick, but you wanted stoutness in a combat knife. Hartung let the bowie balance in his palm, flipping it deftly and catching the soft Kraton handle in a reverse grip. There was nothing like a good knife.

He'd learned to fight with a blade from the men around him. Hand-to-hand wasn't much of a priority in Special Forces, although quite a number of troopers took advantage of their tours in Asia to take up a martial art in one form or another. The war taught its own lessons. He'd listened closely to those who'd been forced to kill with cold steel, their observations recorded and filed away after each debriefing or bull session at the club. Frank knew for a fact that one-on-one knife fighting didn't happen all that often. More than likely you'd find yourself faced with a jammed rifle or a broken firing pin on the old .45. Then it was time to pull that piece of sharpened steel and just plain go at it. The recon teams *sometimes* killed guards with their blades, though the shortened machete was far more appropriate because of its ability to take a man's head off quickly and cleanly.

He'd taken a few lives with a knife. Those memories were painful because the act stripped you of your humanity for just a few vital, life-long seconds. That was war for those on the ground. Kill, or be killed.

"You sure you want to go in there, Frank?" The question had taken him off guard because the answer was so dumb. Sure he wanted to climb into the bunker, how the hell else would they learn what else lay in the enemy complex just over the Vietnamese border? They'd been on the ground for three days now. Chief SOG wanted hard intelligence on the buildup taking place in what was supposed to be neutral territory. After slogging through the dense jungle for seventy-two hours they'd found their first bit of evidence that indeed there existed a major facility across the invisible line that separated one country from the other.

"Sure," he'd told his teammate, "you watch my weapon. I've got my knife and this here flashlight. Shouldn't take but a few minutes and I'll be back." Carefully placing his comrade's hand on the stubby CAR-15 so he'd be able to play watchdog over it, Frank remembered slipping the SOG from its oiled sheath. He'd honed it so fine it would cut you just by touching the carbon steel edge. He didn't really expect to have to use it on another human being. That only happened in the movies.

The bunker was black as a bat's ass. Hartung, his body coated with a sudden sweat, listened hard for any sounds coming from within the earthen fighting position. Nothing. On his belly, with the light in one hand and his blade in the other, he felt for the entrance, finding it and sliding headfirst into the hole. Once inside he waited for a few seconds, knowing the enemy might well be preparing to blow his guts out even as he was praying for the man-made fortification to be deserted.

Still there was nothing. Snapping the flashlight on, he let its beam run quickly over the interior of the bunker. It was clean, he noted, well-maintained, with tins of water, some food, and dug-out shelves on which to stack extra magazines and grenades. The roof was made from thick logs laid into a wide earthen shelf on either side. Sandbags had been carefully laid atop the logs, then a layer of dirt. The camouflage must be superb, mused the reconner, as he checked the floor before taking his first step.

The Cong came out of nowhere. Frank sensed the headlong rush before the impact threw him sideways into the bunker's far wall. He gripped the flashlight and swung it hard as the figure launched itself at him, hands outstretched, fingers bent like an eagle's talons. He heard rather than felt the flashlight connect. A deep grunt escaped from the man's lips, and he rolled off into the darkness before Hartung could stab at him with the knife.

Frank swung the beam around the bunker's interior, catching sight of the VC just as he once again came like a panther up off the hard-packed dirt floor. There was no time to avoid the second attack, nor could he parry with the flashlight. The soldier was in too close, too fast. Dropping it, the sogger grabbed a handful of dank cotton shirt. He dropped rearward and pulled the enemy trooper up and over. He stabbed and knew right away he'd missed the target, because the knife's tip slammed into one of the heavy wooden support beams. Wrenching it free, he spun. The lost flashlight's glow gave off just enough illumination for Frank to see his foe for the first time.

Only the face caught his attention. It was hard, filled with hate, with just enough fear thrown in to give it personality. The man charged again, his lips pulled back so that the teeth glimmered in the defused light of the bunker's interior. Hartung braced himself, the SOG knife held low, its tip toward the ground. As the two men locked in each other's grasp the Special Forces noncom brought the seven-inch blade upward, its sharpened clip ripping a shallow gash in the Cong's upper thigh.

Frank pushed against the man hard. Stomping downward with his boot, he felt his heel connect with the soldier's exposed toes. A tiny cry of pain filled the hole as the man reacted. Hartung followed up with a second and then a third stomping. Pushing forward, he drove the knife forward, feeling it connect with his enemy's body and then sink into it. Grunting and moaning himself, Hartung threw his weight behind the pommel. Charlie was fighting for his life now, his jaws snapping together as he tried to bite the sogger. Both men were locked up in each other so tightly they couldn't have separated had they tried. Frank felt the knife slip deeper into the body cavity, warm blood beginning to run up over the guard and back onto his already sweaty hand.

Then they fell.

Frank lost control, suddenly filled with panic as he realized there might be another guerrilla in the bunker with them. Whipping the knife rearward, he found it was stuck. The suction created by the fluid-filled tissues of the man's wound held the blade deep inside. Hartung jerked at the handle, remembering then to slip his finger over the lower guard while pulling. Suddenly the blade came free, and a horrible sucking sound followed it as Frank drew his arm back and delivered a slashing blow which took the half the man's face off.

A howl erupted from the now-featureless creature before him. Without further consideration the noncom stepped in and delivered a stinging kick to the VC's groin. He got the knee instead. Following up with a stomp to the side of the man's head, he was rewarded with a sharp crunching noise, the skull giving way under the rubber heel's impact.

Frank dropped to one knee and grabbed a handful of black hair. Lifting the semiconscious man's head up, he put the tip of the knife to his throat. As the eyes began to open Hartung pushed the sharpened blade from one side to the other, rolling the body over as he did so, ripping outward once he was protected from the splash of blood he knew was coming.

With a gurgle the thick artery began spraying the body's most vital liquid all over the bunker's interior. The VC's heart was pumping at its maximum capacity. It soaked the dirt flooring within half a minute. Frank, both knees on top of the man's back, simply waited the flood out.

He didn't remember climbing back out of the stinking hole, nor did he later recall finding the flashlight before doing so. There hadn't been any other occupants in the bunker. The dead man had held down a single-man position deep in the jungle so his companions could sleep. The sogger had linked back up with his team. Their extraction took place the next evening. No one asked about his blood-caked uniform until they arrived back at camp.

He remembered burning it immediately.

Frank sheathed the knife and snapped the retention snap firmly in place. It was getting hot now. The sun was up and a harsh glare was already stinging the corners of his unprotected eyes. His belly rumbled a bit, reminding him he hadn't eaten since they'd taken off from the *Midway*. Sucking in a deep breath of warm air, he stood, stretching and shrugging like the old bear he was.

"Hey, Top, you wanna listen to the CNN link? We're bootlegging it off the satellite. Freaking war's over! Bush ordered Stormin' Norman to hold what he's got. We're in Kuwait City and they say it looks like Paris being liberated!"

Frank Hartung waved a hardened hand at the crew chief. "Be right over, son. Just let me grab a ration and save me some more of that coffee if it's still cookin'."

This is my last war, he promised himself as he strolled across the tightly guarded launch site. We get out of this stinking desert in one piece and Sergeant-Major Frank Hartung is going home for good. Gonna take that knothead Thornton with me, too!

"Coffee's on, Sergeant-Major!"

"Airborne!" answered Frank. "And Amen," he finished as he entered the already-humid chopper's belly.

# CHAPTER

# 16

Lee shot the man just as he was opening his mouth to issue a warning to his comrades. The bullet splintered the hard forehead, driving a slippery channel through the soldier's shocked brain and exiting in a balled-up mass through the rear of the suddenly empty skull. Splattered with the thoughts and emotions of their instantly dead companion, the Iraqis behind the second-too-slow point man scattered.

"Down the street to that building with the iron fencing!" ordered Thornton. Bringing his AK to bear, the One-Zero let loose a burst of five quick rounds, punching holes in the street where a thin Iraqi soldier had just crossed at a run. Falling in behind the sprinting men, Bo cursed their luck. They hadn't been on the move for a half hour before bumping nose-first into an Iraqi combat patrol. The gunfight was pell-mell to say the least, men screaming and yelling at each other as rockets, bullets, and grenades were exchanged with less-than-satisfactory accuracy.

Alan Rowe, outdistancing Lee, spun into the open doorway of the building Thornton wanted. His chest heaving, the operator quickly reconned the empty stairwell to his front as well as the length of dark hallway which appeared to run a straight line right out the rear of the structure. Scampering further inside to make room for the team on his heels, Rowe pulled his half-empty magazine from its well and replaced it with a full one. Hearing the solid *click!* of the steel box falling into place, he turned to face Lee, who'd just entered the doorway. "Clear!"

David Lee nodded, jerking his head toward those behind him in a silent signal they could enter. Lee, an active duty Beret, wheezed a sigh of momentary relief. The mission was turning to shit and everyone knew it. First, the confrontation just outside the city's center, now the clash with a second group of goat-eaters. Fighting was heavy, far heavier than expected. The veteran knew it was going to get worse. "Everyone okay?" he asked.

Silver and Bannion gave a solid thumbs-up. Calvin, his back to the team as he covered the doorway, nodded briskly. Thornton, eyes roving the deserted building's interior for any sign of hostility other than their own, acknowledged Lee's "all-okay" with a quick smile which he didn't feel. "We're gonna have to take to the rooftops," he advised. "Street's fulla shooters from both sides. Damn! No one said anything about the amount of troops Hussein's got here!"

Bannion, the RPD gripped tightly in his hands, agreed. "Major push going on. Haven't seen a Kurd yet but there's bound to be a ton of the bastards hanging out. They see us dressed like this and we're in the doghouse big-time!"

Jason laughed outloud, drawing everyone's attention. "I *love* it when a plan falls apart," he giggled. "Shit, let's just get upstairs and do some snoopin' and poopin'. Worse that can happen is we call for an emergency extract and it's home we go. The Iraqis'll just puke if they see a flight of Super Cobras skimming in at treetop level, and our boys will have a field day!"

Bailey agreed. "Upstairs and down a house or two. We run up the radio and see if they've got a fix on Hussein's freq. No go? Then we split."

"Okay by me," answered Bo. "Do it!"

"I'm on point," said Calvin. The former SEAL gave Mike Bannion a hard smile as he brushed past his friend from the Teams, the latter punching him hard on the shoulder in encouragement. Quickly checking his weapon, he started up the stairs. Rowe fell in behind him as a cover man.

Within seconds they were out on the deserted roof, staying low while each took a section to check before bringing the rest of the team up.

"I'm clear here," offered Alan.

"Same-same," returned Bailey. "Get 'em up top and let's head down a few houses. I don't see much activity although you sure can hear it." The sounds of battle seemed concentrated several blocks away from where Calvin was kneeling. Long bursts of machine gun fire, punctuated by the sharp explosions of grenades, reached his ears.

In seconds the team was fanned out in a tight perimeter, everyone looking pleased at being out of the confines of the house. Everywhere they looked, every thing they saw showed the magnitude of the battle for Zakhu. Gaping craters pockmarked many of the buildings still standing, which barely outnumbered those taken to the ground by tank and artillery fire. Bullet holes ravaged nearly every store and house front, window glass was nonexistent except in bitter shards which still hung from their empty frames. Automobiles lay on their sides, most burned, all shot up. Bodies could also be seen. It was a grim reminder of just how unstable Saddam's Iraq was without his iron fist wrapped around the tribal factions' throats.

"Bo? You want us to move a few or just make commo here?"

Thornton checked the AO one more time. They hadn't drawn fire yet, and no one seemed interested in following them since the shoot-out minutes ago. Probably thought they'd made a bad mistake and fired up a squad of their own troops, he thought to himself. "Mike! You and Cal watch our backs. Al! You and Dave spread out and make sure the streets stay clear. Jay? Set your shit up and let's hear what the powers that be have to say about our man Hussein."

Silver slipped his ruck free as the men fanned out to take up the security positions ordered by Bo. Silver unbuckled the straps to his ruck's green nylon flap, slipping them sideways once loose so he wouldn't have to rethread them once the commo check was complete. Grabbing a long-whip antenna, he quickly screwed it into place, snapping the system on and keying the mike twice to ensure it was working properly.

Satisfied with his efforts so far, Jason sat crosslegged on the dusty roof, his weapon in his lap. The E-3 Sentry, or AWACS, was to be monitoring the team's frequency on a constant basis, making ground-to-air communications as easy as a long-distance phone call. Built around the Boeing 707's airframe, the Airborne Warning and Control System was the most sophisticated flying command center in the world. First deployed in 1977, the AWACS was operated by the Air Force Tactical Air Command. Improved in 1984, the new E-C models featured upgraded Tactical Digital Information Links (TADILs) and Joint Tactical Information Distribution Systems (JTIDS). Also improved or upgraded was the plane's radar jamming system and situation display consoles (SDCs). With a ceiling of 29,000 feet and range of 7,475 miles, the AWACS was capable of maintaining a constant presence over the battlefield, vectoring attack aircraft into position and sending bombers to their targets without error. In Springblade's case the Air Force was acting as an airborne command post and relay station, listening in on Iraqi radio traffic so as to RDF Hussein's signals wherever he was operating in the battle zone. Once done, the controller on board would alert Silver to an exact set of coordinates and a time when the signal was received, guiding the team toward their target. At the same time the AWACS was in constant contact with Hartung's crew at the desert launch site. Within seconds it could forewarn the choppers that extraction was required, sending them directly to where the team was using either Silver's team radio or their individual emergency transmitters.

"We're up," Jay told Bo.

Thornton watched his friend carry on a coded conversation with the unseen Air Force controller. The reconner confirmed their position as the plane's electronics targeted them in its computers. Bo couldn't help but compare this conflict with Vietnam. There, the systems had been good, but never as good as this.

Pulling out a pad and pencil, the commo specialist jotted down an eight-digit grid coordinate, which he passed over to Thornton. Leaning back against the open rucksack, Jason glanced around at their meager perimeter. "Yeah, shit's heavy down here. You guys sure about our boy's location?"

Bo was on his hands and knees, bent over his map where he was transferring the coordinates onto the correct grid square given them by the plane. What he got caused him to catch Jason's eye. A broad smile creased his darkened face as the realization of where Hussein was hit home. "Bingo!" he mouthed.

Silver nodded. "You dudes do nice work," he offered. "Confirming we're in A-1 condition although the neighborhood sucks. Two hot contacts so far, no WIA or KIA our side. Estimate between twenty to twenty-five enemy dead. Heavy fighting taking place between the bad guys and the rebels. How copy, over?" Listening intently to the AWACS response, Jason took a moment to pull a stick of gum from his breast pocket. Jamming the sweet stick into his mouth, he began chewing, savoring the sugary juice manufactured by his rapidly working jaws.

"Tell him I have a fix here," ordered Thornton. "Looks like we're less than two blocks from Hussein's hideaway. We might just pull this bitch off yet!" Folding his map back up, the former SOG operator shoved it into the depth of his fatigue pants' cargo pocket.

Silver, who had been attempting to blow a bubble, choked it back and relayed the message upstairs. Their commo complete, he shut down the set, repacked the ruck, and cinched down its straps tightly. "AWACS says they lost contact with Hussein for about a half hour, then picked him back up again but on a slightly different frequency. The operator upstairs figures he changed radios for some reason, or that his command track got nuked because this site isn't moving like the first one was.

"They confirm our estimate of the battle. The colonel's running into stiff resistance from the rebels, who it sounds as if they have been pushed into the northern portion of Zakhu. Our own intelligence is saying the Iraqis are bombing the absolute shit out of the refugees trying to get into the mountains, so the Kurds are giving it everything they've got in an attempt to stall Saddam's ground forces."

Bo's eyes were hard. "They're no match for a pro like Hussein," he spat. "His cousin's got the military skill of a raped ape, but our colonel is a different story. If he secures Zakhu he's got a jump-off point for aircraft and armor, not to mention infantry. The Kurds'll get their collective asses kicked all the way to the border and then some. What a bastard Saddam is! He can't get his licks in against us so he goes for the underdog's throat instead!"

Jason agreed. "Let's not forget our government ain't exactly helping any," he said. "We could have put teams from the Tenth out of Turkey on the ground with the rebels. They could have used AWACS just like I just did to monitor Iraqi troop movements, and simply hit and run all day long. Even better, our boys might have given the rebels some good tactical insight relayed from 'The Bear' on how to seize and hold the major points of tactical interest in northern Iraq. Might be a different story right about now, if you catch my drift?"

Bo had. The downside was they couldn't do a thing about it now. Their objective was two blocks away and possibly moving even as they were sitting on their asses discussing policy. "That's a lick on us," he replied. "Saddle up. We're gonna go get this bastard, one way or another."

Leaving Bannion on the perimeter, Thornton pulled the rest of the team in. He outlined their conversation with the AWACS, leaving out nothing. The men's faces were drawn, hard with anger at what they were hearing. As Special Forces soldiers they were conditioned to cheer for the underdog, to want to see him win. Worse, they knew how to help him do so if just given the chance and logistical support. It went against their grain to have to witness the destruction of the rebels, especially since the Kurds were such tough bastards themselves.

"Okay, so what's the plan?" asked Rowe.

"We use the rooftops to move along, street's fucked up and there's no telling how many Iraqi troops are moving up to support the fighting in the north. We've been lucky, period. One more encounter and someone is going to get nosey and start sending units out to locate us.

"For *once* our maps are good. Hussein is holed up in one of two buildings, either here or here." Bo pointed a smudged finger at two tiny squares on his map. "Figure they'll have security up, but we might be able to bluff our way past most of them in these goat-eater rags.

"Dave? You got the rifle so take Cal as your spotter and plan on covering the rest of us as we make our approach. You get Hussein in your scope, do him. Let us know ASAP so we can backpeddle out of there. I don't give a fuck about bringing this jerk back. We're in the middle of a shit storm and it's going to take everything we've got just to make the Jolly Green, clear?"

Both Lee and Bailey signaled their understanding. Dave was a world-class rifle shot, skilled in the art of sniping and proven on the battlefield. All he needed was a moment's fix on the target and Hussein was as good as dead. Bailey would provide both security for the shooter and an extra pair of eyes when trying to locate the mark.

Thornton continued. "Rowe? You got the point. I'll be your second, Jason's behind me. Mike pulls drag with that RPD of his. We're gonna look for a way in and get a visual confirmation on Hussein. At that point I'll decide whether we blow the freaking building up around his ass, or push him to where Dave can take him out.

"If it comes to us doing the job ourselves, then we'll do it."

Mike spoke up, his question the one everybody on the team wanted made clear. "Bo, are we gonna snatch the colonel if it's possible? I mean, that *is* the mission, ain't it?"

Thornton nodded his understanding. "We open a door and Ali is standing there in his underwear, he's going downtown, period. *If* we can put the cuffs on him, great. Keep in mind that if we're spotted and they put the dogs on us it might just be the colonel's ass anyhow. I ain't leaving him alive, no damn way.

"So play it close and play it tight. We need to watch each other like no time before. And remember the rebels. They have no idea we're in town doing our own thing. You start taking rounds, start punching rounds back. Better we dump a few of them than lose a man trying to be friends, clear?"

"Clear!" they replied as one.

"How about if one of us goes down?" This time the question came from Calvin.

"We bring everyone back. If you think you can't make it, let us know. I'm not going to leave a man on the ground if it can be helped. Shit happens, we all know that. The bottom line is we're a team. So take care of team business should we get pushed that far."

The men looked at each other, knowing what Thornton meant, even if he wasn't saying it out loud. If someone got in a terminal jam he could rely on his buddies to make sure the Iraqis wouldn't have him alive to party with. Total enclosure. It was a bitch.

"Bo!" The urgency in Bannion's voice drew their attention as one to where the big man was kneeling. "We got visitors!"

"Black hats or white, Mike?"

The ex-SEAL breathed an audible sigh of relief. "White," he answered. "Rebel patrol of about eight fighters."

Thornton smiled. "Dave," he said, "see if you can get their attention without getting shot. This might be the break we need!"

# CHAPTER
# 17

The rebels remained clearly ill at ease despite their leader's obvious trust in the words of David Lee. Bo didn't blame the tough-looking Kurds, whose bodies were wrapped in the implements of war. After all, here they were sitting on a rooftop with a band of equally dangerous-looking "infidels" dressed for all the world like the Iraqi sons-of-bitches they were at war with. Strange world we live in, brothers. Thornton turned his attention to Lee, who was talking up a storm with the head Kurd.

"He's convinced . . . I think," offered Lee when the two men stopped speaking.

"Nice work. How'd you get him to buy off on these glad rags of ours?"

Dave laughed, the rebels ignoring him as they listened to their leader explain the Americans' mission to Zakhu. "Thank God I went in with the Tenth," he said. "While we were setting up launch sites and all that crap I got the opportunity to meet up with a bunch of the Resistance people. You know the right names and doors open. This guy's name is Saad. He's a midlevel chief for his clan, been fighting the Iraqis ever since they started picking on the refugees. He knows Zakhu well, as well as the back of hand. His people bring their animals and crops here to barter and sell, or at least they used to."

Bo was overjoyed at their break. Now they might be able to get around without looking in every nook and cranny along the way. Plus, if the Kurds hung with them, the overall battle strength of the team was almost doubled. More firepower meant a better chance of pulling the mission off. "What's he doing now?"

Lee moved a bit closer. "Saad speaks our language, although he hasn't let on yet. Most educated Kurds do, just as the Iraqis. Right now he's letting his men know what's going on, who we are and why we're here. They'll vote on whether to back our play or just leave us to our own devices. I'd feel a whole lot better had the President sent in the calvary once the shit hit the fan for these people."

The rebel leader held up his hand, stopping all talk within his group. Turning, he motioned to David who in turn tugged at Bo's dirty battle-smock. "Showtime, Boss."

"We will help you locate the animal Bush has sent you for," stated the fierce-looking rebel. "The butcher's kin is the key to this battle. Without him we may in time take the town back. My men are still ill-at-ease. The uniforms and weapons confuse them."

Lee waved a hand at Mike who was laying on his belly several feet away, watching the group's meeting intently. "Bannion! Whip that rag off your head a minute and let them see what a Viking god you are!"

The Kurds' eyes' opened in disbelief as the commando's thick blond hair dropped to his massive shoulders. As one they began talking, pointing with fingers and unsheathed knives at the revelation. One moved quickly to where Bannion was, carefully touching his hair in frank amazement. With a laugh he spit a rapid burst of speech to his friends.

"What's the buzz?" asked Mike, his eyes on the rebel's hand as he continued to stroke the giant's hair.

"They're convinced," chuckled Dave. "Your new friend has a lot of weight with his buddies and he's telling them you can't possibly be an Iraqi scumbag with hair like that!"

The rebel tugged at the former SEAL's headgear. "Now what?" quipped Mike.

"He wants to rewrap your 'patrol cap' for you. Let him. It's a sign of trust and good faith."

"Bitchin'," growled Bannion as the Kurd deftly tucked and spun the cloth around his head. "Just as long as he doesn't have a sister he wants me to meet."

As the earlier tension melted away the two groups mingled. Saad assigned a rebel to each of the Americans, doubling up with Thornton and Lee, who now assumed the command element for the group. "The streets are filled with Iraqi soldiers," advised the Kurd. "We have been fighting further north, but many groups are infiltrating back to the south to mount attacks against Hussein's rear elements.

"The building you want is the town's police station. It is two levels in height, with a basement. The windows are barred, the interior very modern with thick doors. It is a natural command center and well known to the Iraqi pilots who fly the helicopters."

Bo grunted. "Fort-fucking-Apache, huh? Can we get in from the top if it comes to that?"

Saad nodded. "There is a door and passageway. He has a way out the back as well, which we can cover now that there are more men. I have no more rockets for my RPGs, so if there is armor we may have a problem."

"We'll tell the men to keep an eye out for any abandoned rounds or a dead gunner," said Lee. "I'm silenced on the rifle so if push comes to shove we can kill the vehicle commanders if they're outside. If the colonel is using the station as a C&C center he'll be wanting to ring it with as much firepower as available, just for his own sake."

"True," remarked Thornton. "Let's get it on, then. We leapfrog the rooftops until we're close enough to get a visual on the area. Dave, you and your group will move out and select a site for the rifle. Saad and me will wait til you're in position before kicking the door. Anything out-of-step comes up before we split the team, we'll talk about it then. Clear?"

"Roger that. I'll get them cranked up."

Saad waited until Lee had begun passing the word before speaking to Thornton. His English was indeed good. "Sergeant, why is it that Bush helps the Kuwaitis but leaves the Kurdish people to reap the devil's wrath?"

Thornton had expected this to come up. He'd heard the question asked before, first from his "Yards" in Vietnam, when it was certain the United States was going to pull out and leave the losers to the fury of the victors in the North. Later he would hear it asked again by the Salvadorans, when financial aid and support was being threatened by the Congress. America had a bad habit of abandoning its most trusting supporters, all in name of policy. "I will not pretend to know the answer to your question, Saad," he began slowly, "but I will speak from my heart because you have combined your fate with ours."

"It is enough," commented the Kurd.

"My country's people are very concerned about being in your part of the world. We do not understand your ways, nor do we truly want to. Many, many sons and daughters have been brought to fight Saddam in Kuwait. Their families will accept their deaths in that country, because it was seized and brutalized by an outside force. Bush feels they will not accept the loss of their loved ones if they fight in Iraq."

The rebel's eyes showed no emotion at Thornton's words. "Do not the American people understand we also fight for our country?" he asked. "The Kuwaitis are a rich people, an arrogant race which cares nothing for those outside its borders. Is there democracy in Kuwait? No. Is there freedom in Kuwait? Again, no. Only oil and the value of its position next to the Gulf.

"The Kuwaitis will only rebuild their nation after this war is ended. They will build it exactly as it was before, with only the Emir and his family in power regardless of the lies and promises he is making.

"It is good that the United States and her friends have fought against Saddam Hussein. But it would be better if you continued the fight, cutting the head of the snake off and destroying all he stands for in this land called Iraq."

"One day that may be so," offered Bo.

"The day will pass!" snapped Saad. "The Kurdish people heard the words of your President over our radios even as Baghdad was burning in the night. 'Rise up!' urged Bush. 'Throw off the chains of your captor and we will support you!'

"We did as your President asked, Sergeant. My people took their weapons and came down from the mountains. We took the towns of the north without resistance, driving the Iraqi forces before us, losing many fine fighters but conquering the land!

"Then we waited for your planes to help us as Saddam dispatched his tanks. We waited for your paratroopers as the infantry once again moved forward. We waited for your President to keep his word to the Kurdish mothers and fathers whose own sons and daughters were dying for democracy.

"He did not come!"

The afternoon's heat was blistering, its waves washing over the roof-bound group like a sea of fire. Concrete dust and cordite stung Thornton's eyes, the aftermath of battle a reminder of the destruction each side was determined to inflict, win or lose. The Kurd's words stung his soul. No, Bush hadn't done more than offer his best wishes as the rebels gave it their best shot. It was like urging a small child to cross a busy intersection against the light. What would most likely happen was a given. It was unforgivable. It was murder. It was a habitual action for America's policy makers. Well, he thought, at least we're being consistent.

A smattering of rifle fire broke out behind their position. All the men rolled to their bellies out of combat instinct, rifles and grenade launchers at the ready as each sought out the origin of the exchange. As its intensity grew the Kurds began jabbering back and forth. "What the hell is going on?" asked Alan.

"We are mounting a counterattack in Hussein's rear," exclaimed Saad. "It is a diversion to make him pull his troops back from the front. We have many Kurds trying to flee. If they cannot get deeply into the mountains soon the Iraqis will catch them with their tanks and armored cars. The helicopters are bad enough, spilling acid down among the people as they seek shelter, machine-gunning them without mercy, rocketing them without remorse."

The American Special Forces man simply stared at the ground in shame. How could they let Saddam's murdering scum get away with genocide like this? Why hadn't Schwarzkopf told the President they could go all the way? What would it have taken? A week? Two? The Kurds would have swept the Iraqis from the north even as Saddam would have ordered them back to defend the capital. The Republican Guard forces were proving to be an overblown band of scoundrels, the Twenty-Fourth and "Big Red One" devouring them in the south. With only easy-to-kill Hinds flitting about, the Air Force ruled the skies. Their body count was the highest in recorded history for such a short campaign. Leave Saddam in power? It was a war crime in its own right!

"I apologize for our inability to see the truth," said Bo quietly. "I fought in Vietnam, again in Latin America. I would have hoped our eyes would be more fully open this time. It is to my shame and sorrow they are not."

The Kurd's eyes widened for a moment, then assumed their bulletproof depth as Saad weighed the words of this strange warrior in his land. "I feel the truth of your words in my heart," he said after a moment's contemplation. "There is honor in what you say. I also acknowledge the fact you and your men are here, deep within the belly of the beast just as we are. If any of you die we shall bury your bodies deep so that the animals cannot feast upon them. I accept your presence and we shall fight alongside each other as brothers."

"Bo?" It was Lee. "Best take advantage of the hoopla going to make tracks for Hussein's hideout. One of the Kurds spotted some movement up top about two blocks west of us. I got a feeling we're gonna see some serious shit start flying unless we put a boot in it now."

"Roger that," said Thornton. Hitching up his harness, the big commando checked the safety on his assault rifle, locking eyes with Saad even as the Kurd did the same. Indeed they were brothers, bound together by a common thread of humanity if not cause. Besides, he liked the bastard. "Okay, Saad, let's go find Saddam's ugly little cousin. Your boys look like they need to kill a few more goat-eaters before the sun sets, and I'm a little bitched off myself about the whole thing."

"Sergeant?" replied the Kurd as they began loping across the rooftops. "We also eat goats."

"But you're *good* goat-eaters, my man," chuckled Bo. "There's a big difference."

The Hind swooped down from the sky like a hawk. As the rockets dropped free from the chopper's pods, the guerrillas vainly tried to find enough cover on the grassy slope to escape their blasts.

Haziz lifted his AK and tried to align his front sight on the roaring aircraft. It was a good place for the Iraqi pilot to make his attack. The long rolling slopes of the high country were devoid of rock outcroppings or deep ravines. The best the rebels could do was find a shallow depression and hope the Hind would be satisfied with half their number dead. Squeezing the trigger, the Kurdish leader began sending tiny darts of copper toward the chopper. His body came apart at the seams as the nose gunner ripped him from stem to stern with a laserlike blast from the mini-gun.

More Kurds were dying now. The Hind slipped away and then turned, only a few inconsequential holes in its frame. Heavily armored, the Soviet-made airship was meant to do just this kind of work. The rebels were easy pickings out in the open. Their infantry weapons were no match for the firepower carried by the Hind's crew.

Soon it became a game for the Iraqis. Assured by their squadron commander that the Americans would ignore their presence in the air, the Hinds were flying mission after mission against the rebellion. It was a joke, of course.

The few fixed-wing fighters still in Iraq were grounded; the Americans appeared out of nowhere to shoot them down when they were discovered off the tarmac. But the helicopters flew without concern, dumping their loads of bombs and mines along suspected travel routes, pissing acid upon the heads of the women and children fleeing the destruction of their towns and villages, machine-gunning the dogs who dared raise a weapon against them.

Like these curs below, thought the pilot.

Soon enough it was over. From the air their bodies looked like broken stick figures. Tiny pools of bright red blood stood out from the green grass like checkers on a checkerboard. Weapons were strewn around, thrown away as the rebels' lives were snuffed out. There would be no burial for the dead. Their flesh would be left to feed the wild dogs which roamed the hills at night. To the Iraqis it was just another day of killing the enemies of Saddam Hussein, ungrateful citizens of Iraq who should have learned their lesson long ago.

As the Hind turned for its new base at Zakhu it conducted one last low pass over the killing ground. The crew congratulated itself on their day's pickings, already telling lies about how many they must have killed. The lies would grow larger once they'd landed to refuel and rearm.

High overhead an American F-15 requested permission to engage the enemy aircraft scooting along the earth's surface more than seven thousand feet below him. Denied authorization, he pounded the inside of his cockpit in frustration, then turned the jet around and headed back to the *Midway*'s flight deck.

# CHAPTER
## 18

Colonel Hussein clucked his tongue at the stupidity of the Kurdish rebels. *Imagine*, he thought, as he surveyed the battle map in front of him, *imagine how fruitless an attack they are mounting when I have three Hinds inbound already?* The radio reports of massed rebels once again assaulting from the south had caused only a brief few minutes of confusion before Hussein was able to react. Ordering his forces north of the town to continue their advance, he then mandated those in the southernmost portion of Zakhu to dig in and stop the Kurds seeking to distract him. The gunships would work their deadly magic among the ranks of the mountain clans, scattering them to the wind and relieving the unexpected pressure at his rear.

"Colonel? Your new track is ready and the tank escort is here as well."

"Excellent!" barked Hussein. The ringing in his ears was all but a buzz, the cuts and bruises from the destruction of his first command track forgotten. They'd nearly got him, the hairy bastards! But they hadn't and that was going to work against them as the battle for Zakhu was concluded. "I'll be out in a moment, corporal. Ensure the area is clear of any snipers or rebel suicide squads. I don't relish being made a martyr of the revolution."

"Sir!" cried the soldier, then he was gone.

Hussein straightened his tunic and checked the pistol at his side. His beret was gone, a battlefield loss due to the close encounter he'd suffered earlier in the day. In its place was a standard-issue patrol cap loaned him by one of the senior captains who'd scooped him up as the street fight intensified. A bit tight, it fit none the less, and the colonel was pleased.

There'd been a coded message waiting for him after he'd cleaned up. Saddam was recovering his normal high state of emotional well-being after learning the forces against him were going to stop short of taking all of Iraq. The rebellion was now the primary concern of the president. The rebels in the south were being forced across the border into Iran, with Iraq's second largest city, Basra, in ruins. The destruction was unavoidable, and Saddam in truth wasn't concerned. It could all be rebuilt using petrodollars.

That was the punch line of the entire joke, mused the colonel. By leaving his cousin in power, the allies were doomed to be put to the economic sword somewhere down the road to Iraq's recovery. Seven times the country had been conquered in her long and glorious past. Seven times she had thrown off the yoke of her oppressors and become a power to be reckoned with.

The Americans were a constant source of surprise to Ali. First they lament about being beaten by the military midgets of North Vietnam, a country which relied solely upon the logistical power of the Soviet Union and Red China to sustain her war effort. Gutted by the experience, the United States wallowed in self-pity until offered the opportunity to beat up on the island of Grenada and then Noreiga's Panama. Hussein had been more concerned than many of his peers about *these* little excursions. He'd noted the attempts at combining the joint forces, the problems which were reported and the subtle adjustments made by the American military as they refined their methods and machinery. It was not their military might which had stunned the colonel during the debacle of Kuwait, but rather the hard-line political stand Bush had been able to muster as well as the sweeping support of the American people for their soldiers.

And now they were screwing up their chance at a total victory.

Rolling up the map he then stuffed it into a leather document case. No matter the insanity of the politics, it was his job to crush the rebels in the north just as his counterparts were doing so in the south. Had the Shiites been successful, as well as the Kurds, Iraq would have become a collection of feudal states. That was what made Bush's decision to hold back *any* support for any one side a wise one in the midst of forgoing a complete military rout.

The Kurds wanted nothing more than their own little kingdom in the north. As a force to replace Saddam they weren't interested, nor would they have been able to assume such a position had they been. Not a great group of people to count on if you were the United States.

Iran's Shiites were far more capable of promoting a political solution to the void which Saddam's departure would create, but again, the United States could not hope to influence the government of Iran to moderate whichever puppet leaders it installed in Baghdad. Economically crippled by the eight-year war, the Iranians could well use the vast oil fields of a conquered Iraq to rebuild both her civilian as well as military economy. Bush could not afford that much power to be refined through the cunning government of Teheran.

Which left who? There was no credible opposition to Saddam Hussein in Iraq because, quite frankly, the president had killed them all off long ago. None of the Arab countries aligned against them were in the least bit interested in dominating Iraq with all its problems, nor would they lend their support to any country in the region who might be stupid enough to think about doing so. Israel would no doubt *love* to annex both Jordan and Iraq if offered such a long-shot opportunity, but that in itself was such an inane proposition that the colonel dismissed it with a chuckle.

No, Iraq under Saddam was at least a known factor. The allies would justify their position by the logic of the "big picture." His cousin's base of power was untouched; the military was only decimated in the south where forces had been deployed to Kuwait. Much of the army was intact north of Baghdad and along the Iranian frontier. Syria had never posed much of a threat on her side of the border, a fact which had as much to do with the terrain as with any other consideration the Syrian commanders might have pondered.

Damn Schwarzkopf for having the balls to flank them through western Iraq! The colonel had to give the American officer much credit for that move.

"The men await you, Sir. The field commanders are reporting great success in the north with many, many rebels counted dead."

Hussein grabbed the briefcase and headed for the door. By nightfall he'd own this forgotten little town; the rebels would have been broken into groups which could be mopped up as time went on.

There was no use hanging around what remained of the police station.

"Fire!"

The Kurds opened up in a withering burst of assault rifles and grenades which dropped Iraqis in the street where they had been preparing to evacuate the temporary headquarters of their colonel. Resupplied with a rucksack full of rockets for his RPGs, Saad carefully lined up one of the Russian-made tanks and let loose. The roar of the launcher was swallowed up as the rocket's tiny motor kicked into gear, propelling the warhead, which impacted directly between the tank's turret and main body.

A monumental explosion rent the air, sending huge chunks of shrapnel flying. The tank went up in a ball of flame and smoke. Bodies littered the street as the ambush continued. The command track of Colonel Hussein erupted into bright yellow and red flames as a second, then third rocket plowed into its lightly armored shell. Two other tanks began backing down the street in opposite directions as their commanders realized how easily the rebels were taking the steel coffins apart. Guerrillas with rockets on rooftops were sheer death for the tank crews, whose machines couldn't manuever within the tight confines of the town's roadways.

The Kurds let them flee.

"Here we go," yelled Thornton. With a leap the street fighter cleared the rooftop adjoining Hussein's command center, landing hard on its tar-paper surface and rolling out of the way of the rest of the team. An Iraqi trooper spun around at the sound of their intrusion, his rifle held low as he took in the fact the men were wearing the same uniform as his.

It was a fatal mistake.

Rowe pounded out half a magazine's worth of lead into the man's unprotected gut. The rounds tore him in two, spinning the upper trunk one way, the lower portion of his body the other. Leaping to his feet, the Springblader sprinted for the doorway leading to the interior of the station, all other guns on him as he slammed up alongside the hot concrete structure. "Come on!" he yelled.

Silver and Thornton were next, running as a team. Their weapons were held out in front of them in the classical assault stance, snouts sweeping the open rooftop. Bannion and Rowe covered them at both ends. Mike was next. The burly SEAL scrambled to his feet just as a burst of fire ripped up the ground around where he been laying. Firing a fast burst of ten from the RPD, the commando snaked across the roof while his teammates put up a wall of protective fire.

"Get-the-fuck-inside!" ordered Bo as Mike rammed his way through the group at full speed. The wooden door gave way; its hinges were pulled clean out of the wall. Bannion took the point, and the team clambered down the dimly lit passageway, each man careful to stay out of the others' lines of fire.

Outside the firefight was heating up. Lee was shooting Iraqis as if there were no tomorrow. One after another he dropped them. His vantage point on the third floor of a building opposite the station gave him a commanding view of the area. Next to him lay Bailey, who was watching their backs and wishing he were absolutely somewhere else. He'd killed two goat-eaters so far, both of whom had shown the poor sense as to try and flank them. The Kurds were holding their own, slapping more lead downrange than Calvin could imagine coming from any one unit their size. It was a slaughterhouse in the street below, with the carnage continuing as more Iraqi soldiers were sent out to do battle.

"Team's inside!" yelled Lee just as he torched another Iraqi in an upstairs window.

"Goodie," answered Bailey. "Now all we got to do is wait until they grab the dumb-ass and reappear. I see many more Indians coming down the warpath, pal. Better see some help soon or we're gonna have to grease the colonel right here and now!"

# CHAPTER
## 19

"Frank! Better shag your ass over here! Your RTOs on the horn and it sounds like we're in business!" The site commander waved a hand at Hartung, who was playing his third round of poker with the crew of the MH-47. He'd won about $400 so far. The aviators were far better fliers than card players.

"Start premission checks, boys," he told them while stuffing the deck back into its cardboard box. "If Bo's got Silver cranking on the telephone you can bet they're either hip-deep in a world of shit or ready to come home empty-handed." Walking quickly across the hard sand, the retired sergeant-major privately guessed it was the former rather than the latter option. Thornton would only have had enough time to get into the city by now, which meant they were compromised and in contact with the Iraqis or that the team had done the job on Hussein.

"Here's the message," offered Colonel Craig. "Just came in relayed from the AWACS. What do you make of it?" Craig was a hard-bitten mustang colonel with Task Force 160. He'd personally asked to ramrod this mission, knowing it was a major op at the tail end of a very quick war. His command had so far performed superbly, justifying the crashes and deaths the squadron had compiled during their months of training and preparation for just such a deployment. Craig wanted one last bit of frosting on the cake, knowing it would be some time before his boys would once again be given the chance to prove their worth.

Frank read the decoded slip of paper. Sweat ran down his face as he did so. *Damn! Looks like the rules have changed one more time.* Staring at the colonel, Hartung crumpled the note in his hand.

"Bad news?" Craig asked slowly.

"Could be better," answered Frank. "But then, it could be worse."

"So where the fuck are we?"

Hartung grabbed a stool and sat. The colonel joined him. The launch site began to hum with anticipation. "Bo's in contact at the grid coordinate given him by AWACS earlier. They're fighting tanks and armored personnel carriers as well as Iraqi infantry. Jay says they're being supported by a band of Kurds, where the hell they ran into them only God—or Allah—knows.

"Thornton wants us airborne. He's asking for immediate air support from the Cobras around the building. Also, he wants to extract the colonel *if* he's found by STABO."

"STABO!" spat Craig. "That means sending the bird in under fire. Don't know how the crew will respond to that."

Frank allowed the officer a moment to reflect, then continued. "Bo'll let us know the score before we're on-station, count on it. He says they'll fight their way out with the rebels and meet us at the primary PZ unless it's been compromised. Then we'll head for the alternate. Knowing my partner like I do, he'll send a man up with Hussein on the rope, just to get *somebody* out alive."

The colonel stood, rubbing his short hair with a dirty hand as he surveyed the activity going on around them. It wasn't supposed to have gone down this way, but then, what plan worked perfectly anymore? "I've got to contact 'The Bear' and ask permission to provide air-to-ground support with the Cobras. The cease-fire is in effect and sure as shit the Iraqis will raise hell about our boys churning up the earth in violation of the terms once we begin pouring hot brass down their pants."

"You'll get it," assured Hartung. "They want this toad too badly to back off now just because we need to do some daylight gun runs. Get your permission and I'll start rigging the STABO."

Craig waved a hand and shook his head. "Nawww, let's just do it and take the fallout if and when it comes. I'm not going to take the chance of some REMF acting in Schwarzkopf's best interests, ordering me to stand down when your man is depending on us to show up for dinner.

"You talk with the Jolly Green and I'll brief the Cobra crews. The rangers can provide a squad for security if we need it at the PZ, the rest will stay here and man the fort til we get back. Don't count on us hanging around here for long, though. Once we extract your team and pick up my headhunters, it's a flat-assed race for the Saudi frontier, brother!"

Frank snapped a salute. "Fine with me, Sir!" Spinning on his heels, Hartung loped across the compound, thinking to himself what might have happened to make Bo decide to take Hussein out alive. Obviously Lee wasn't given a clean shot at the man or he would have been dead. Plus, there *was* a war going on in Zakhu but no one but the team knew just how bad of one. If Thornton was allied with the Kurdish rebels it meant he'd needed more horsepower to get the job done. That meant Hussein must have been located but found to be impossible to remove without an all-out assault.

"We going after your buddy, Top?" The crew chief, his sunglasses firmly in place against the day's glare, met Frank halfway to the waiting helicopter.

"Roger that, young man. Get the STABO gear out and let's rig it! We're gonna jerk our POW off some damned roof if I've got my hunches right . . . and in full view of half the Iraqi army!"

Together the two men began opening boxes and uncoiling the STABO's line. The rest of the crew were already in their flight suits, the chopper's engine beginning to turn over as the pilot started his preflight checks. A squad of rangers ran up, their faces streaked with camouflage paint, their bodies draped with an astounding amount of ammunition and weaponry.

"Where you want us, Sir?" asked the sergeant in charge.

Frank pointed at the Jolly Green's empty interior. "Inside, boys. We're yanking a goat-eater under fire while the Cobras spray the shit out of Zakhu. From there we head for a PZ where—God Willing and the creek don't rise—we'll find my teammates and a bunch of Kurdish rebels. Any questions?"

"No, Sir!" snapped the noncom. "In fact, Sir, it sounds like a piece of cake!" With a brutal smile the ranger ordered his men into the MH-47 at the double.

*Always liked them boys*, reflected Frank. *Good buncha lads when the chips are down.*

He hid his face as sand began flying, the Cobras already airborne and making a practice pass out in the desert to check their guns.

It was killing time again.

# CHAPTER
## 20

"Message received and choppers inbound!" Jason Silver jammed the handset into the outer pocket of his ruck and gave Thornton a huge smile despite the growing amount of gunfire outside.

"Great job, Jay. Remind me to put you in for a medal when we get back. In the meantime, let's get ready to grab Hussein should he still be alive and in one piece." Bo dropped his AK's magazine, inserting a fresh one and chambering an equally fresh round. The others checked their own firepower. Bannion dumped the second empty drum of his RPD. "Everyone ready?" asked Thornton.

"Let's do it!" spat Rowe. "I'm on point."

Alan threw a quick look down the hall and then began running its length for all he was worth. The rest of the team fell into place, spacing themselves out as much as possible in case someone didn't take to their being on the premises. Caution was thrown to the wind. The reality of the situation demanded aggressive action. Better to be lucky than good, the man had said. And it was true.

Somewhere in the building was the butcher of Kuwait. Bo Thornton was going to find him and either kill the Iraqi officer, or send him skyward to Frank Hartung.

And you could take that to the bank.

Hussein was once again crawling on the floor. All around him were dead and wounded soldiers. Some of them were crying, others were cursing the rebels, whose attack seemed never-ending. The colonel himself was wounded. A throbbing pain came from his lower leg where a round had entered it after bouncing off the marble floor. He'd tied a strip of cloth around the gaping hole, jerking it tight to stop the flow of blood. The surviving tanks were gone, leaving their dead comrades to witness the destruction of the station, as the Kurds once again intensified their attack.

Upstairs! Pulling himself along, the officer grabbed hold of a rejected assault rifle whose owner was nowhere to be seen. Climbing painfully up the wooden stock, he braced himself against the stairwell. His eyes rolled up into his head as he almost fainted from the effort. Where were the reinforcements? The radiotelephone operator had gotten an urgent plea for help out just before a grenade had destroyed his position. If only they could hold out for a few more minutes Hussein was sure they'd be rescued.

Hobbling up the stairs one at a time, he urged himself not to cry out. He could feel the blood beginning to run again as he put weight on the damaged leg. Its dark wetness seeped out from beneath the bandage and ran down his once-polished boot. The AK's barrel slipped once on the stone surface of the stair, almost causing the colonel to lose his balance and tumble back down from where he'd come.

But he caught himself, more out of sheer will than anything else. The climb continued. Hussein reminded himself how poorly he would be treated if captured by the rebels. There was no doubt in his mind his cousin would leave him to rot in whatever prison they'd shove him into. Saddam wasn't concerned with hostages, even those from his own family. The man had *shot* some of his relatives, for Allah's sake. Once the word got back to Baghdad that Colonel Ali Hussein was a prisoner of the Kurds they'd just give him a medal for trying and go on about the business of rebuilding a greater Iraq.

So much for blood being thicker than water.

He was almost at the top of the stairs now. There seemed to be firing going on from the second level but he couldn't be sure. They'd placed several Iraqi soldiers up here to protect the rooftop; it was obviously those men who were valiantly fighting off the rebels from their fortified positions. If he could just find one of the men and have him care for the officer's wound, things would be better for the moment.

Hussein stepped into the hallway; his eyes flared open and he threw a hand out in a vain attempt to ward off the oncoming body of one of his men. The two collided with a sharp *smack!*, and Hussein passed out even as his head bounced off the corner of the wall. Alan Rowe tumbled after him, and his rifle clattered off the floor as he rolled halfway down the stairwell before catching himself.

"You okay, Al?" asked Bo, kneeling with his AK at the ready.

"Sure, just a few more bumps and bruises to write home about," answered the former Green Beret. "Toss me my shooter, will ya?"

After doing so Thornton rolled the unconscious Iraqi over, whistling as he recognized their target's now-passive features. "Jackpot! Old Alan just tackled the colonel hisself, boys!"

Mike Bannion scooted up beside his team leader, confirming the man's identity by jerking the officer's ID passbook from his unbuttoned breast pocket. "We're good to go," he said. "Says right here this is Colonel Ali ibn el Hussein. I can't believe our luck, gentlemen. Someone here has been living the pure life."

"Tie him up and drag his ass back down the hall!" ordered Bo. "Al! You hold off any Indians wanting to find higher ground while we make contact with Frank." The Chinese-American gave a hard thumbs-up, climbing back up the stairs and laying flat on the floor so he could cover the still-empty stairwell with both rifle and grenade.

Thornton was halfway down the hall when he spotted Jason. "Get the radio up and let's see how far they are out. I don't think there's many bad guys left downstairs, but you never know."

"How about letting Dave and Cal know we got our man?"

"Good idea," answered Bo. Jerking his emergency radio from its case on his combat harness, the One-Zero punched in a number and waited for the triple-beep which meant he'd made a connection.

"Pizza Delight, what's your order tonight, Sweet Thing?"

"Always the asshole, right Cal? Tell Dave we got Hussein and the choppers are inbound. How you guys doing over there?"

There was a pause, then Lee was on the line. "Turkey shoot, Bo. We just got reinforced by about fifty Kurds from Saad's side of the family. The Iraqis are pretty much holed up underneath you guys from what we can tell. I figure maybe another ten minutes worth of last-ditch effort and the Kurds will rush the station. How are you doing?"

Thornton passed the news on to Silver, who relayed it to the snatch team. Cheers echoed down the hall from both Bannion holding the rooftop, and Rowe at the stairwell. "We be mighty fine," he said. "Hussein's alive but wounded. He's not much to look at for being such a badass, but then most of us ain't when we're down and out."

Lee chuckled into the tac-phone's mouthpiece. "You gonna hook the bastard out?"

Bo finished tying a cravat around the colonel's leg. He'd wrapped it twice with Ace bandages, then covered the elastic mass with a field dressing. He was pleased to see no sign of seepage once it was all in place. "STABO. Should be easy now that the rebels control the immediate area. I'm worried about a rocket up Frank's ass, though."

"We'll get some of Saad's people on the flanks and rooftops. I doubt there's going to be much incoming for at least awhile. The Kurds are ready to exfil to the high country, they've made their point and bought what time they could for the refugees."

A burst of hot automatic gunfire ripped through the building, and the sound of booted feet was cut short as war cries exploded from the mouths of those rebels breaking in from the rear of the station. Screams of pain and pleas for mercy rolled up the staircase; the Iraqi voices were subtracted one by one until only the rough language of the Kurds could be heard.

"Bo! You guys okay in there!" Lee's voice held an edge of murderous concern to it.

"Yeah, the calvary just evicted the Indians from the premises, that's all. Alan's gonna make contact *very carefully*, so we don't get our asses shot off by mistake. See if you can't get Saad over here to ease the introductions. You know how we all look alike in these goat-eater outfits!"

"Will do, Boss! Want us to hold our position or move across the street?"

Thornton pondered the question for only a moment before answering. "Get your mangy asses over here, Dave. We might all go out on the bird and I don't want you waving goodbye should more of Saddam's lovable losers show up. I wanna take Saad and some of his people out too. We can drop them near the mountains, maybe give them a better chance at continuing the fight than if they have to E&E outta here."

"We're on the way, out here." The line went dead as Lee shucked the phone to Calvin, already loaded up and waiting along with two rawhide-tough Kurds who'd been assigned to guide the two operators safely across the street.

Thornton mouthed a silent prayer to the man upstairs. It looked like they were going to pull another one off, and he was pleased as punch to see it.

After all, they were good . . . but they were lucky too.

# CHAPTER
# 21

Hussein's last command post was a hive of activity. Those Kurds wounded during the assault were being cared for on the main floor, which had been turned in to a makeshift aid station. First aid bandages and medicine were those taken from the bodies of the dead Iraqis, the rebels having nothing other than their prayers to comfort the injured. Small cries of pain echoed throughout the building as the men were attended to. The bodies of those dead or dying were simply covered and left for someone else to bury.

Upstairs the mood was somewhat different as Thornton's team prepared the colonel for transport. Silver, his radio now set up on a scarred desk once belonging to the chief of police in Zakhu, was talking with Hartung, who was on board the MH-47 with the fast-approaching extraction team. It had been decided the Cobras would work out their guns on a tiny perimeter set up around the captured building in order to help hold any Iraqi reinforcements at bay. David Lee and Mike Bannion were coordinating the gunship strikes, using their handheld tac-phones while they observed the surrounding area from the roof of the station.

"Tell that old fart to have the Jolly Green swing its big ass around and drop the ramp," explained Bo to his RTO. "We'll on-load the colonel's stretcher, then ourselves right from the roof. It'll be the team, Saad, and ten of his people. From here we fly out to the mountains where the rebels will unass the 47 and we'll hook for the launch site to refuel and grab the rangers. Good copy?"

As Bo turned away he eyed Saad, who was sitting quietly, staring at the drugged form of Colonel Hussein as the wounded man lay strapped onto an improvised stretcher. The Kurd reminded Thornton of a holy man, his features impassive as he contemplated the thing of evil at his feet. Crossing the narrow hallway, the Special Forces operator turned his back to the wall then slid down its rough facing until he was sitting Apache-style on the cartridge-strewn floor of the ravaged office. "He'll live," was all Bo said.

Saad nodded slowly. "So many of his victims did not. It makes me wonder about the scheme of things, why Allah would allow such a creature to survive when so many innocent lambs lost their lives at his spoken word. What will happen once you return him to Kuwait?"

Thornton pulled his patrol cap from his head, rubbing greasy hair with an equally oily hand. He wanted a shower, bad. Then a decent meal and a pot of fresh, hot coffee. His body ached with fatigue, its innermost tissues stressed and strained from the exertion of the day-long gun battle as well as from the pounding march of the night before. He'd found at least three rock bruises where he'd fallen or collided with something, and most of the others were equally as tired and/or marked with similar minor cuts and scrapes. Maybe it's time I began counting my blessings as well as my money, he thought. Saad's question returned to him. The man was patiently waiting for an answer.

"He will stand trial?"

"This is the plan as I understand it," said Bo. "We are to turn him over to the Kuwaitis as soon as an official representative of their government returns to the capital. From that point on it is out of our hands, although President Bush very much wants him to pay for his crimes against the Kuwaiti people in a public forum."

"And of his crimes against my people? Will these be

brought before the world at his tribunal? Will I be taken to Kuwait to testify as to his involvement and guilt in the genocide of the Kurd?"

"I don't know, Saad. Certainly I can mention it when I return and am debriefed. The Kurds have an equal case against Hussein, this the world knows by now. Your plight along the borders will draw the interest and attention of the media; that will announce your cause and concern to the nations of the coalition."

Saad pursed his lips and was quiet for a moment. When he spoke his voice was relaxed, as if the two men were sharing a lunch at a streetside cafe. "I know to what I shall return soon, but you, where do you go to, Sergeant?"

Thornton smiled as he pictured Linda's face in his mind. "Home to my wife, my friend. We have a house high atop a bluff overlooking the ocean. I haven't seen either since the war began. That's where I'm going, back home."

The rebel touched Bo gently on the shoulder, the message clear. "Good. It is good you are returning to your own country and family. I, too, am making the same journey. But I'm afraid our homes will be the camps for awhile. Saddam Hussein has evicted us from our towns and villages. The people are afraid to return, they remember the poison gas, the tanks, the aircraft. Already his troops have begun leveling our houses and shops. He wants us to know he can control our lives like a farmer controls his livestock. It will be many days before I can truly return to the land I love and call mine."

Thornton returned the hardened Kurd's gesture of understanding with one of his own. This war was no different than any other he'd fought. The ones who most needed help seldom got it in time. The tribes and clans and minorities who threw their lot in with Uncle Sam were the ones who paid for their allegiance with everything they owned and held dear, including their lives and the lives of their children. It seemed it was Bo who was always going home when others had to stay behind and pick up the pieces of their shattered lives.

"Bo? Gotta check our man here. Frank's only ten mikes out and he's wanting an update. How're you doing?" Alan Rowe's face showed the man's concern.

"Okay, just tired like the rest of us. Me and Saad been talking about what's going to happen after we drop him and his boys off in the mountains. Go ahead and get the creep's vital signs, we wouldn't want anything to happen to him after all that's gone down."

Standing, both men left the filthy confines of the ruined room to allow Rowe some space as he made sure Hussein was resting comfortably. Climbing the short flight of stairs leading to the rooftop, the two welcomed the sun's decline as dusk began to take hold of the town. Firing could still be heard from distant parts of Zakhu. The first of the Cobras was making its initial run against a target of opportunity spotted by its pilot. Tiny explosions followed the hammering of the armed chopper's guns and rockets.

"Ammo, or maybe a fuel dump," commented Thornton. "Seems the colonel has plans for Zakhu as a staging area against your people, Saad."

"As Allah wills it, it will be so. I think you are right, Sergeant."

"Oh," said Bo. "About what?"

The guerrilla squatted, saying a few brisk words to one of his own soldiers and then waving at Calvin Bailey, who was sharing a smoke with a thin Kurdish rebel armed with a loaded RPG. When his attention had returned to Thornton his voice was soft, like the darkness coming on. "The world will see our plight this time. Hussein's war was too big, too cruel for all it touched to be ignored. When the reporters come to our camps we will show them the wounded, the hungry, the sick and the dead. We will bring them to the children crying for the lack of milk. We will tell them of the horrors of travel in the mountains, of the butchers in their helicopters, of the ambushes and robbery by traveling bands of human jackals.

"We are a proud people, my friend. Our struggle to be free has lasted for years against this man. When I was in school I studied your country's revolution against the King of England. Your people fought also, against great odds and for several years. Americans only wanted a homeland of their own, a place where they could live as free men. The Kurds want nothing more or nothing less; won't the world see that if they visit our misery along the borders?"

Thornton sat quietly. The distant sound of inbound helicopters made its way through the smoke and haze of the battle. Soon Frank would be guiding their airframe in on the infrared chem-lites Mike Bannion was already nailing into the surface of the roof. Would Hussein live long enough to stand trial? Most probably. Would the Kuwaitis convict him? It seemed certain. Would they make him pay for his crimes and the greater crimes of his cousin? That remained to be seen.

"This is my last war, Saad. Been fighting for over twenty years now and I think it's time to hang up my guns and settle down, once and for all."

The rebel smiled. "It must be a good feeling inside to know you can make such a decision and keep it. I, too, will one day trade this rifle for a more peaceful tool. My heart wants nothing more than to enjoy a simple life, but until my people can share a lasting peace in our own land I will continue to fight."

"Inbound and Frank says he ain't waitin' on us!" Jason Silver—his rucksack packed, slung, and cinched down— came bounding out of the shattered doorway where Bannion's bulk had torn it free during their combat entrance. "Bo, we gotta go. Alan's got some of Saad's boys giving him a hand with the colonel and Frank's last message was for us to prepare to board."

Coming to his feet the night fighter was once again in command. "Saad? Time for us to boogie outta here. Please get the men you want to come with us and tell them to make sure their weapons are on 'safe' before they load the chopper.

"Jay? Get our people in tight and keep an eye on them, I don't want to have to count noses more than once. From the sounds of it the Iraqis are getting their shit somewhat together, and I'll just bet we're gonna see an armored push back into this section of the town now that they know their president's kinfolk is in the hands of the rebels."

"The Cobras are reporting heavy concentrations of troops and vehicles in the southeastern sector. They're afraid to fly much closer than they are already, too much of a chance of being brought down by antiaircraft fire."

Bo watched as Saad began gathering up his cadre. "How bad you want to get back to the coast, Jay?"

The question took the man who was one of Bo Thornton's closest friends by surprise. "As bad as anyone who's been stuck over here on a freaking boat for seven months can want," he answered. "Why, what's on your mind, Boss?"

Thornton watched as Mike carefully snapped the hard plastic shells of the chem-lites in his powerful hands. He knew Frank would have his NVGs on, making it a simple task to spot the PZ from the air. It would be a hot load, the chopper barely touching the rooftop as its human cargo was loaded onboard. The Cobras were working in close to the station now, their turbines sounding like massive hornets as the two-man gunships hosed down entire streets with their firepower. There wouldn't be many Iraqis trying too awfully hard to retake their little oasis, thought Bo. Not with the steel carpet of firepower the Cobras were laying out.

"Bo, you were saying?"

The rest of the team gathered around the One-Zero, their attention on him as the Jolly Green's huge airframe swung into view in the last remaining bits of sunlight left in Iraqi airspace. "I got something to say, gentlemen, and not much time to say it.

"We're gonna deviate our course a bit to drop Saad and his people off. He's taking his field commanders and medical team, RTO and at least one translator. They need the head start if they're gonna outrun Saddam's assholes.

"You've all done one hellva job. I've run a few teams in my time but never one as good as this, and I mean that.

This war was worth coming to because we had a good cause and the support of the American people behind us. It ain't been that clear-cut in the past, it ain't gonna be in the near future.

"As of the moment Frank touches down I'm calling it quits. But before I go home to Linda there's got to be a detour along the way. Saad's people are needing help, lots of it. I think I'm gonna tag along with him and see if perhaps I can't spend a bit of time building instead of destroying. That's what the program's all about anyhow, at least it was when I first joined up to win the beret."

The double downdraft of the chopper began to pick at them, whipping sand and surface grit from the roof and throwing it hard against the men's exposed features. Looking upward they could see Frank's dim form leaning out from the lowered ramp, a taut monkey-strap keeping him from doing a nosedive to the street below. They'd be airborne within minutes.

"If you don't mind some company I think I'll tag along," said Jason. "Ain't that much I'm going back to. Hell, Linda can run the gallery for a few more weeks without my mucking up her decisions!"

"Up to you, Jay," said Bo. "I wouldn't mind the company but it's your choice."

"I'm in," said Silver. "Can't break the team up this late in the game."

"Me, too." Alan Rowe stepped forward, his face lit up with a huge smile. "Uncle Sam don't own me no more, he lost all rights when I ETS'd years ago. Been awhile since I humped a ruck for the fun of it. You two don't mind the company, I'm joining up as well!"

"Suit yourself," laughed Bo, slapping the stocky soldier hard on the shoulder.

Bannion spoke up, the tone in his voice clearly giving away what his feelings truly were. "Bo, me and the other guys would love to tag along but . . ."

"But you're still formally in-service, Mike. I know that and so do the rest of us. I want you guys to ensure our scumbag buddy Mr. Hussein gets back to Saudi in one piece. I've a feeling he's going to prove to be more of a headache than he's worth, but that's the coalition's problem."

"Take care, big man," ordered David Lee. "See you when you've worked it all out for yourself."

"Thanks, man."

Bailey stepped up just as the chopper began its descent. "You're a bad motherfucker, Thornton. I'll tell Conrad to send the final checks . . . and I'll see your big ass on the coast in a month or so, right?"

"Roger that, squid."

"Get the fuck on board you buncha gold-brickin' legs!" Frank Hartung's voice lifted above even the scream of the MH-47's turbines, its welcome sound breaking the moment's spell as they all hurried to climb aboard.

Two weeks later—

A soft coastal breeze lifted the curtains by the open sliding glass door, bringing in the smell of the ocean. Frank Hartung took a deep sip from the coffee cup in his hand, watching the beautiful woman who was Bo Thornton's wife. The man who knew her husband better than anyone else hadn't been a bit surprised when he'd watched the big bastard jump off the ramp, Silver and Alan Rowe right behind. It was exactly what Frank expected of his friend, so he hadn't argued or tried to change the former One-Zero's mind.

He'd just shook hands and passed some more ammo out the door.

"How's the coffee?" Linda Thornton turned away from the platter of eggs and bacon she was preparing for their breakfast. A tall brunette with a high-caliber body, she was a far cry from the young girl who'd captured Thornton's heart when they'd met so long ago.

"Perfect," complimented Frank. "Finally slept all night. Been awhile." Hartung accepted the full plate handed him. Grabbing a fork he dug in, enjoying the rich taste of a home-cooked meal.

"He pisses me off, you know."

"Would me too, just that I take it better after all these years."

"He could have been killed trying to reach the border. They all could have been killed." Linda sat, her full breasts rising and falling as her breathing accelerated with her concern.

"But he wasn't and they weren't. I imagine there's a few more Iraqis gone to Allah, though. Your husband was a good asset for Saad's 'Pesh Merga,' they needed a few more guns on their side to make that last mile home."

Linda smiled. "Pesh Merga. 'Those who face death'. Been Bo's whole way of life hasn't it, Frank? Facing death I mean."

Hartung nodded, washing a mouthful of egg down with some coffee. "It's the warrior's creed, honey. They can kill you, but they can't eat you. The professional soldier—which is what Bo is and always will be—has to accept the fact that his life is already taken. Once he does that he can balance his fear, use it for the better, ride it like a mustang.

"It's the fearful man who is doomed to die like a coward on his knees. The warrior accepts his fate and steps forward, always careful not to tempt fate because that's a fool's path. But he never runs from it. Yeah, your old man's a warrior and he is following his faith. He'll be home soon, count on it."

Linda covered the old veteran's hand with her's. She'd grown to love him like a father, to trust his insights and to listen to his words. "What about you, Frank?"

He laughed, the sound bringing a smile to the girl's face. "I'm running point for Bo, Lin. Always flew covey for him anyhow, so it makes sense I be the first to hang up the hardware and turn in my boots. I'm fine, fit as a fiddle and ready to enjoy my second retirement to the fullest!"

"Will Bo and the others be home soon? I miss him, Frank. I miss him with all my heart."

Standing, he moved slowly around the table to wrap his powerful arms around the gently sobbing woman who was his comrade's wife and friend. "He said to give him a month to rebuild the humanity the war sucked away from him. He wants to help feed the hungry ones, he wants to use a hammer and nails instead of a gun and knife.

"He wants to come home whole again to the woman he loves more than life itself."

"I'll be here for him when he does," murmured Linda.

"Airborne and Amen," Frank whispered back. "Airborne and Amen!"